AMAZON HORROR CRUISE

ERIC S. BROWN

SEVERED PRESS
HOBART TASMANIA

AMAZON HORROR CRUISE

AMAZON HORROR CRUISE

Winston McKay ran for his life. The corridor that surrounded him was narrow with burning torches placed along it every twenty feet or so. Gillyman's screams echoed off its stone walls from far behind McKay, the sharp cracks of the mercenary's pistol having fallen silent.

McKay's breath came in ragged gasps as his legs pumped beneath him. He was pouring on all the speed his body could muster. His eyes were wide in terror. He heard Gillyman let loose a final, wailing cry and knew the mercenary was dead. The creatures were likely feasting on him . . .at least those of them that weren't already coming after him. McKay had ordered Gillyman to buy him some time. He knew his goal was close. If he could only reach it before the creatures caught up with him, McKay thought, then. . . then he'd be able to save himself. It had cost him over a decade of his life and almost the entire fortune he'd inherited from his father to find this place. There was no way in hell that McKay was going to let the pack of hungry creatures on his tail stop him from reaching his goal now. Rounding a bend in the corridor, he saw that the corridor up ahead opened into a huge room with a high ceiling and knew that something had to be done to further slow up the creatures that were after him.

He couldn't allow the creatures to stop him from reaching his goal. McKay stopped, whirling around. In the white knuckled grip of his right hand was a .357 Magnum. He wasn't a soldier like Gillyman and his men had been but McKay knew how to shoot. McKay had known that coming here would be dangerous but he hadn't expected there to be so many monsters!

Raising his .357, McKay waited, taking aim at the bend in the corridor. The thing that came around the bend in the corridor was shaped like a dog but its eyes burned a bright red in the dim torchlight. A row of jagged spines ran from the back of its neck to the base of its tail. Razor-sharp fangs gleamed within its snarling mouth. The beast's foul eyes fell upon him and McKay felt his heart skip a beat inside his chest. It was all McKay could do to hold his pistol steady as he squeezed the trigger. The Magnum thundered. The creature staggered backwards as the high-powered bullet slammed into it. Not giving the thing a chance to recover, McKay fired two more shots in rapid succession. Putrid, black blood exploded from where they struck the creature's body. It stumbled sideways and then collapsed.

McKay heard more of its kind coming. . .a hell of a lot of them from the sound of it. Gillyman's violent and bloody last stand must not have thinned the creatures' number as much as he had hoped it would. With only three rounds left in his .357, McKay had no option but to return to his mad flight for the room that lay ahead.

McKay sprinted into the room ahead of him. His headlong run became a stunned sort of stumbling across the stone floor as he saw the elevated throne on the opposite side. Upon the throne rested a skeletal figure, slightly slumped over, a large spear clutched in its right hand. McKay didn't give a damn about the spear or the skeleton itself, what he had sought for so very long was the dark jewel in the center of the dead man's crown. It was real, not that he had ever really had any doubt, and within his reach. McKay could hear the vicious snarls and fierce, howling shrieks of the creatures drawing closer. There was no time to do anything but rush the throne and hope that there were no booby traps to prevent him from reaching it. He ran up the steps of the elevated platform where the dead man sat upon the throne. McKay's skin was drenched in sweat and his throat was intensely dry. It almost seemed impossible that he had finally found the Obsidian jewel that so much of his life had been spent searching for. His hand shot out, snatching the crown from the skeleton. The movement knocked the dead man's head loose from the top of his neck. McKay didn't even notice the skull that went bouncing down the steps. His entire focus was upon the Obsidian jewel as he clutched the headband crown tightly, staring into the swirling darkness that swam within it.

One of the creatures came bounding into the room. It skidded to a halt, red eyes glaring up at him where he stood on the steps in front of the throne. Two more of the things came bursting in behind it. McKay's trembling hands raised the crown to his head and he put it on.

Together, the three creatures charged up the steps towards him as cold pain wracked McKay's body, soul, and mind. As the world before his eyes went black, the last thing he saw was one of the creature's open mouth, razor teeth gleaming, as it leapt at him, intent upon tearing out his throat. The scream that escaped McKay shook the entire room.

****

The convoy of Jeeps and trucks roared along the winding road. Dr. Emma Wallace bounced in the passenger seat of the lead vehicle. Marcus Brutan, the "C.O." of her hired guns and personal bodyguard, sat next to her in the driver's seat. His face was a scowl of frustration and determination as the big man kept his eyes glued on the way ahead of them. The convoy had already lost two of its Jeeps to the rough state of the road but Emma was just glad there was a road to where they were going. Many places this remote along the Amazon were only reachable by boat and she knew they were close now. If her estimation of things was correct, the small port village of Parin should be coming into view soon. Emma had never been able to find the village on any official maps of the region. She suspected that very, very few knew it even existed but it did.

The village was the last place that her college mentor, Dr. Winston McKay, was known to have been before simply vanishing from the face of the Earth. The two of them shared little in common these days except for an all-consuming drive to find the lost Jewel of the Tlayoalli. McKay, the bastard, had always seemed to be several steps ahead of her. Had he finally found it? All Emma knew for sure was that her own research led her to believe that as the Aztec Empire fell, a group of priests fleeing the Spanish carried the jewel deep into the jungle and hid it there. It was difficult to believe that McKay hadn't re-emerged from the jungle to lord his discovery over all those who had mocked them for even believing such a thing could exist if he had indeed gotten his hands on the jewel. Emma was pulled out of her thoughts as Marcus grunted.

"There it is, Dr. Wallace," the big man nodded his head forward.

Emma's breath caught in her throat, eyes blinking, as she saw the village. The place was little more than huts and wooden houses, raised upon rough looking beams to keep them from being damaged by floods. The houses and huts alike were mostly topped by thatched roofs. There were two, larger, more modern buildings. One of them was clearly a bar, the other resembled something akin to a warehouse retrofitted into living quarters. Beyond the village, at its other edge, was the flowing water of the Amazon River. From the looks of things, there appeared to be perhaps a few dozen people who lived in the village at most. What truly caught her eye though was the boat secured to the village's dock. It appeared to be both a mesh of things that were both outdated and cutting edge high tech. The boat surely wasn't military in nature but was nonetheless, she suspected, armed to the teeth. There were wicked looking machine gun turrets at its bow and stern. Armor plating lined its hull. Not a single smoke stack or radio tower protruded upwards from the boat. It was sleek shaped with a slanted bridge that raised up from near its center closer to its bow than stern. The boat looked fast, agile, and violent. And Emma knew she was likely going to need it.

Marcus brought the truck they were in to a stop. The other trucks and Jeeps of the convoy pulling up behind them to kill their engines as well.

"You ready for this?" Marcus's deep voice rumbled as he withdrew the truck's keys from its ignition.

"As I'll ever be," Emma frowned. "Best we get to it."

Emma swung her door open and jumped down from the truck's cab. The soles of her boots made a crunching noise as they landed on the gravel of the road. The air was muggy and hot. The midday sun was burning brightly in the sky above. Emma used the backside of her hand to wipe sweat from her forehead and then took a look around.

In total, there were two trucks and three Jeeps in the convoy. Marcus was already out of their truck too and barking orders at his men. The inhabitants of the village, at least those who hadn't run and hid upon as the convoy pulled up, stood around in small groups, watching them all closely. Some of them wore modern clothing, shorts and simple T shirts, but others wore red skirts or nothing at all. Several were armed with spears and two held bows which thankfully weren't drawn or aimed at their group.

Murphy, a thin, geeky man, who was Marcus's interpreter, hurried to talk with the gathered crowd. He spoke in Panoan then Arawak, and Carib. No one from the crowd responded though several of them were now smirking at Murphy.

The crowd parted as a giant of a man clapped his hands loudly and moved through it towards them.

"No need for all that, my good man!" the giant exclaimed with a smile. "We all speak English here. You are American, yes?"

"Yes," Marcus answered, moving past where Murphy stood, straight towards the approaching giant. Reaching into his combat vest, Marcus withdrew a photo, holding it up. "We're here to find this man. Supposedly he passed through this village some time back. Do any of you remember seeing him?"

The giant laughed. "But of course we've seen Dr. McKay. He came through here as you say. The man is of the sort that is hard to forget. He spent a great deal of money during his short stay. A complete nut job though, was obsessed with getting a boat to take him down the river in search of some lost relic."

Emma couldn't hold herself back. She rushed

towards the giant, eager to press him for more details on exactly where McKay was headed, how long ago he'd departed, and if the villagers had seen him since then. Marcus reached out, clasping her shoulder to her back, stopping Emma.

The giant laughed again. "I can see that you very much want to know more. We can certainly help you in that regard but first. . .Let's get you all settled in. Margaret over there owns the inn that we built for the river traffic that passes through. Get rooms from her and we shall meet again for dinner to discuss things more."

As the giant turned to walk away, the crowd dispersing around him, Emma called out, "Wait!"

He stopped, turning to look back at her.

"I'm Dr. Emma Wallace. What's your name?" She smiled, excitement and hope pouring out of her.

"Quinaametzin but you may call me Quin. Most do," he answered.

"Quin, does that boat at the dock belong to the village?" Emma asked.

Quin snorted. "No. It does not. The vessel belongs to Captain Eli Richards."

"Is he here in the village currently?" Emma pressed.

With a deep sigh, Quin said, "It is easy to see that you and your people will be seeking his services. I will invite him to dinner this evening as well. Perhaps he'll come. We shall see."

Emma wasn't happy with Quin's answer but knew it might be a bad idea to push him more than she already had. She looked to Marcus to take the lead on what was needed to be done next. As large as Marcus was, Quin was even bigger. As primal of a warrior as Quin came across as, Marcus still seemed the more deadly of the two. If Quin wasn't on the level, Emma didn't want to think about what Marcus and his mercs would do to them.

Marcus's group consisted of over a dozen men and women with all sorts of varied backgrounds, most ex-military. His second in command was a young woman by the name of Rachel. Marcus left her with a squad of others to watch over the trucks and Jeeps as everyone else headed for the inn that Quin had directed them to. Murphy was one of the few that lacked the hardened, combat vet look that most of the others had. The other seemingly less violent members of Marcus's group were Tali, Chris, and Froggy. Tali was the group's medic. While she seemed just as fit and tough as any of the other soldiers, there was an air of compassion about her. She always had a smile on her face and often hummed upbeat tunes. Chris was the group's tech guy. He was both an engineer and a computer nerd, overweight enough to fit the stereotype that went along with being as smart as he was too. Sweating profusely in the midday heat, Chris kept grumbling under his breath about the sun and how burnt he was going to be tomorrow. And finally, there was Froggy. He was a lanky young man with short cropped black hair who was the group's communications expert.

The soldiers that stood out to Emma in the group were Dan, Haus, and Nadja. Dan was strange to her. He was both a priest and a soldier. An average looking guy with a gray specked beard, Dan always wore a small silver cross about his neck. In many ways, he was as much the group's counselor as Tali was its medic. If you needed to talk, he was there, ready to lend an ear. During her own brief conversations with Dan, Emma had discovered that he was a very educated man in addition to being a man of faith. He was well spoken, charming, and a warm spirited guy who seemed to sincerely care about everyone.

Haus on the other hand was something else altogether. He wasn't overpowering in demeanor or intimidating like Marcus but the man was built like a brick house. Emma had nicknamed him Tank in her own mind. Stocky, beefy, and burly, Haus wasn't any taller than she was, barely five six in height. His voice was like a roll of thunder when he spoke, rumbling and deep . . .and from what Emma saw, Haus didn't speak often. When he did, even Marcus listened to him. Haus was among the oldest members of Marcus's group with the scars to show that he had earned living as long as he had. The man didn't skimp on his personal weapon choices either. Haus carried a huge minigun, its belt running from the heavy pack of ammo on his back into the weapon. But that wasn't all Haus was packing. The burly, little man wore a holstered, pump action shotgun on his side too and knives strapped to his boots. If the crap did hit the fan somewhere along the way, Emma was dang glad that Haus would on their side of things.

And then there was Nadja. The woman wasn't strikingly beautiful but neither was she in any way average. Nadja was the sort of lady who could blend into or stand out in a crowd by choice. There was no doubt that she was just as fit as any of the others in the group but her hips and arse were full, enough to be called plump. She was agile and fast despite this, way faster than she looked. In addition to the standard issue sidearm that the majority of Marcus's group wore holstered on their hips, Nadja always carried two hatchet-like weapons on her hips. Emma had seen her practicing with them on their journey and it was an impressive sight. Nadja's hair was long and jet black like a starless night sky and always pulled back into a tight ponytail. Nadja's eyes were a bright shade of green that betrayed her mental sharpness. Emma couldn't figure out if she liked the woman or not, supposing though it didn't matter. Nadja was just a hired gun in her service like all of Marcus's group.

The four members of the group who stayed behind with Rachel to watch over the trucks and Jeeps were Alex, Chad, Brian, and Olivia. Emma didn't envy them. They'd be stuck out in the heat and sun while everyone else was headed inside where surely to goodness there would be air conditioning.

Marcus led everyone into the inn that Quin had directed them to. Margaret was waiting for them at the small desk in the foyer. The air was much cooler and crisp, lacking the mugginess of the day outside. Emma shivered in pleasure at the feel of the cool on her skin.

Margaret greeted them with a smile, wearing a low cut dress that showed off the ebony curves of her breasts. "Welcome to our humble village. How many rooms will you be needing?"

Emma glanced over at Marcus, not really knowing the answer to that question.

"One for Dr. Wallace and another six for my personnel," Marcus said.

"Only six?" Emma asked, confused. Counting him, there were thirteen people in Marcus's group.

"We'll be rotating in shifts," Marcus gruffly explained. "Six will be all we need. Besides, if things go like you're hoping, we'll be on the river by tomorrow."

Emma nodded. "You heard the man. Seven rooms total please."

After payment was settled and dealt with, Margaret handed over seven sets of keys to Emma. They were old school, real old school, as in put it in the lock and turn it. The layout of the warehouse turned inn was odd but easy to navigate. There was only a single floor. Emma saw Haus and Nadja entering the foyer from one of the two corridors that led out of it. She hadn't noticed them leave but knew what they'd been up to. The old vet and Nadja had been checking the inn out for trouble.

"Place is like a Hardened Site, sir," Nadja flashed a grin. "Easily sealed up and locked down tight."

"It's clear, too," Haus rumbled. "At least of anything obvious."

"Should be a good place for us to hole up and let the doc take a gander at her comics," Nadja added.

Emma frowned. She hated some of the jargon

military folks liked to use, knowing that Nadja was referring to her maps of the region. Even so, she couldn't argue about them being called comics too much. There weren't any official maps of the region that were helpful. So much of the area was nothing more than river and jungle. The maps she had were mostly things she had sketched out herself from satellite imagery, ancient historical texts, and legends.

Marcus passed out the keys, handing Emma's to her first. As the group of mercs went off to find their rooms, the big man headed back over to the desk where Margaret was still watching them with a smile.

"You know what strikes me as odd?" Marcus huffed at Margaret.

"What's that?" Her smile held but Emma could tell the woman's defenses went up.

"My man Haus over there is carrying around a fragging minigun in your inn, hell, all of us are armed and look like killers, and yet. . . none of that appears to have freaked you out in the slightest, Margaret," Marcus challenged her.

Margaret visibly relaxed some. "Oh, Mr. . .?"

"Let's just stick with Marcus," he said through scowling lips.

"Well, the answer to that question is really simple. The man you're searching for, this Dr.

McKay, he brought a bunch of soldiers with him as well. Out here, armed men and women are the norm when it comes to people passing through our village, whether they are political rebels, hunters, river pirates, or folks like yourself. So far, nary a one of them has bothered me. I suppose they don't consider an innkeeper and native woman like myself a threat," Margaret's smile returned.

"And are you?" Marcus asked.

"Am I what?" Margaret teased, knowing exactly what he had to mean.

"A threat, Margaret," Marcus frowned.

"No one in this village is. . . unless you make us one," Margaret warned.

"Understood," Marcus nodded. "I just like to know where things stand."

"Don't blame you," Margaret chuckled. "I am much the same. Now, why don't you retire and get some rest with the others? Dinner is not far away."

"I don't think so," Marcus grunted. "But thank you for your time, Margaret."

"My absolute pleasure, Marcus," Margaret batted her eyes at the big man.

He walked over and asked, "Dr. Wallace, would you like me to escort you to your room?"

"You know you're supposed to call me Emma, Marcus. We haven't been strangers for some time," she grinned. "But no, I believe I can find it on my own."

"Call if you need me then," Marcus told her. "I'll be outside getting things in proper order with the vehicles and our supplies in case your hope for tomorrow pans out."

Without waiting for her to answer, Marcus stomped out of the inn. Emma watched him go and then headed off to find her room to get cleaned up a bit before dinner. Their first impression upon this Captain Eli Richards was the most important thing to her right now. They needed him and his boat badly. Without it, they would be stuck here until either another boat arrived or they came up with a new plan on how to reach their destination.

Emma's room was very modern. It contained a bed, a mini-fridge, a tight closet, and a table that could fit two people at it. There was an adjoining bath, that was plain and simple. Emma hadn't realized just how tired she was. The bed was very alluring. Her mind was wound up and Emma knew even if she tried to grab a short nap, there would no rest gained from it. What she really needed before dinner was a shower. Emma wanted the sweat of the day off of her. Stripping off her clothes, Emma headed into the bath. The water felt like heaven, flowing over her skin. Afterwards, Emma got into a fresh set of clothes, shorts and a loose shirt, then left her room in search of Marcus.

****

Rachel and her squad stood guard over the trucks and Jeeps. She quickly saw it was a pointless task. The villagers had lost all interest in them after Marcus led the others away to get rooms at the inn other than a few who occasionally approached them to offer food or water. The people in the village seemed like good folks. Their mix of appearing primitive and modern somehow at the same time was mind boggling to Rachel. It was like they were doing their best to hold on to who they were while realizing that in order to survive, they needed to adapt to the outside world that was slowly encroaching upon them more and more every day.

"That's one heck of a boat down there, boss lady," Chad commented, gesturing towards the boat secured at the dock below the village.

"She does look pretty killer," Brian chimed in.

"Boys," Olivia chuckled. "Give something a bit of tough looking armor and some guns. . ."

"Doesn't matter what the thing looks like," Rachel shrugged. "What matters is can it get us where we're headed?"

"Yeah, and where exactly is that again?" Brian laughed.

Rachel shot him a stern glare. It was hellish enough to be standing around out in the heat without Brian's jerk, flippant comments adding to it.

Chad walked over from where he stood near the lead truck to punch Brian in the shoulder.

"Hey man!" Brian cried out, rubbing at where Chad's fist had hammered him.

"Brian may be a prick but he's got a point, ma'am," Chad said. "We don't really have a clue where we are going, do we?"

"That's not something we need to know, Chad," Rachel reminded him. "And frankly it doesn't matter. Our job is to protect Dr. Wallace and make sure she makes it in and out of wherever the heck we end up."

Chad reached into his vest, digging out a pack of cigarettes, and lit up. He didn't challenge her on what she said. He just shrugged half-heartedly at her answer and let it all drop.

"Rachel!" Marcus's voice boomed as he called to her, emerging from the inn.

She snapped to attention as he approached them. "Sir!"

Marcus frowned at her. "You're not in the army any more, Sergeant."

Rachel relaxed a bit, her cheeks flushing. "Old habits die hard."

"That they do," Marcus agreed, holding out his hand to Brian. "Let me have one of those."

Brian hurriedly handed over a cigarette and his lighter.

"I thought you quit," Rachel chided Marcus.

"I thought so too," Marcus shrugged. "This gig. . ."

"I get it," Rachel nodded, "It's sure not the norm."

"No, it isn't," Marcus took a big drag on the cigarette. "I don't like being so cut off out here. Something goes wrong. . ."

"There's no help coming," Chad finished for him.

"That's the job," Marcus huffed. "Same old, same old, the only difference is. . ."

"What?" Rachel asked. "Don't tell me you think that we're really going to find this magical do-dad she's after and it turn out to be real, do you?"

"Monsters," Chad grunted. "Where there's magic, there's almost always monsters."

Rolling her eyes, Rachel sighed. "There is no such thing as real magic. And how the heck would you know if there are always monsters around magic anyway?"

"Ha," Chad grinned. "I do read and watch movies, ya know?"

"He's right about there always being bad things around magic in movies and books," Brian chimed in.

"Gentlemen," Marcus called them down. "This is the real world. I didn't say anything about monsters. I think we have enough things to deal with on his one without making crap up in our heads."

Alex finally joined in the conversation. "Pirates. That's what I think we're going to run into. I mean look at that boat we're trying to get. Do you think it's armored and weaponed-up like that just to look cool?"

Marcus nodded. "Pirates are certainly something we need to watch out for. There have always been pirates in these parts and they've only gotten worse as the modern world, its drug gangs with it, continue to push into these regions."

"I want to talk with that boat's captain," Rachel said. "If anybody knows what we're really headed into, he'll be the guy."

"You're welcome to," Marcus told her. "It looks like our stuff is going to be just fine where it is."

Marcus looked at his watch. "He's meeting us for dinner shortly."

****

The village's bar was more like a tavern, with a

very restaurant feel. It was well air conditioned though dimly lit. The sun was setting outside and its final, fading rays shined weakly through the place's few windows. Marcus had wanted to bring quite a few of his people with them to ensure her safety but Emma had ordered him to keep their party small. It consisted only of Marcus, his second in command – Rachel, Murphy, and herself.

Quin was waiting for them near the door as they arrived. He led them inside to their table. There was no sign of Captain Richards.

"I can see you are wondering where Eli is, my dear doctor," Quin smiled. "Fear not, he will be arriving shortly. The man sometimes like to make . . . an entrance."

Quin clapped his hands and their dinner was brought to them by the inn's servers. Emma's plate was set down in front of her. It smelled heavenly. Emma hadn't realized how hungry she was. The first thing she noticed on her plate was a mound of Bolinho de Macaxeira. It was most commonly served as an appetizer and was certainly making her mouth water. Made of cooked manoic mashed and stuffed with cheese, deep fried in oil, Emma relished its taste, popping a ball of it into her mouth. Her plate also contained a side of Chonta salad. It was the heart of raw palms cut into strings like fettucine and seasoned with local spices. And finally there was the main course. It was Patarashca, fish grilled with a mix of veggies including onions, chilies, tomatoes, and coriander wrapped in a large bijio leaf.

Rachel and Murphy seemed to be just as impressed and happy with the food as she was. Marcus wore a scowling expression, continually looking around, as if he was expecting trouble. The big man never let his guard down. Emma couldn't blame him. It was his job and what she was paying him for. Still, Quin and his people were friendly without any signs that she could see at least of anything sinister up their sleeves.

Emma caught herself; she'd started eating before anyone else, including their host. Her head jerked up, eyes wide, cheeks flushed red to see Quin smiling at her.

"Ah, Dr. Wallace," His smile grew wider, "I do like a woman with an appetite."

Quickly wiping her mouth, placing the napkin back onto the table, Emma apologized for her bad manners. "I. . . I am sorry. Please excuse me."

Quin laughed loudly. "There is nothing to forgive, Doctor! In fact, I take your action as a great compliment to my people."

"Thank you," Emma did her best to match Quin's smile with one of her own.

"Is that him?" Marcus grumbled, interrupting them.

Quin's eyes darted towards the door. A man of average height with a sleek build, wearing a cockpit jacket and red glasses had entered the tavern, heading in the direction of their table.

"Eli! I am so glad that you could make it," Quin shouted, rising from his seat at the head of the table. The giant rushed forward to clasp the hands of the man in the cockpit jacket. Eli nodded at him before Quin released his hands. Following Quin back to the table, Captain Eli Richards took a seat next to Quin, facing Emma and Marcus.

Just before Quin and the captain had reached the table, Marcus had leaned over to Emma, whispering, "The captain looks rather hungover, does he not."

Captain Richards's head was inclined in her direction as he sat down but Emma couldn't see his eyes through the strangely red lenses of his glasses. Even so, Emma's instincts told her that the captain was checking her out. She didn't know whether to be offended or not. Despite the captain's aloof, put off-ish swagger, there was a charm about him and he was rather good looking in an "everyman" kind of way. Emma was quickly beginning to write the captain off as just another guy who could be swayed by any halfway attractive woman who batted her eyes at him. It would make getting his boat a lot easier if he was.

Settling in at the table, Captain Richards reached for the margarita that was waiting for him at his spot, taking a chug from it, then unexpectedly got straight to business. "Quin tells me that you people want my boat."

Marcus started to answer the captain but Emma laid a hand on his arm, silencing him.

"We do," Emma forced a smile. "Our friend, Dr. McKay, passed through these parts some time ago. We're attempting to locate him."

Captain Richards laughed. "That's a crock of crap."

"Excuse me?" Emma stared at him.

Emma saw Marcus's hands clenching into fists where they rested on the table top near his plate.

"Come on, lady," Captain Richards smirked. "We both know what you're really after. There's no need to play games."

"Watch your tongue," Marcus rumbled.

Emma was frowning. She hadn't hired the big man to protect her honor.

Before she could say anything more, Captain Richards leaned forward. "You're after the Jewel of the Tlayoalli."

Blinking in utter surprise, Emma jumped as if startled by his words.

Captain Richards laughed again. "I knew it."

"How could you even know about the jewel?" Emma demanded.

"I'm not an idiot like your buddy Dr. McKay is sweetheart," Captain Richards chided her. "There's not exactly a lot of things that would bring people like you to this region."

"The jewel is only a myth," Quin spoke up. "Everyone here knows that. It is a tale told to give children nightmares and nothing more."

"Nightmares?" Emma balked.

"The word Tlayoalli translates to meaning darkness in your language, Dr. Wallace," Quin explained. "But I am sure you know that."

"I do but. . ." Emma started.

"My people believe the jewel is a thing of pure evil," Quin said. "But as I said, thank the spirits, it is not real."

"But she believes it's real, Quin," Captain Richards took another swig from his drink. "And so did that McKay idiot. Doesn't matter if it is or isn't, folks like them will always be chasing it."

Emma huffed. Now sure that she didn't care for the captain at all despite the eccentric charm in his appearance.

"Doesn't matter what any believes in terms of the thing being real," Marcus jumped in. "We're searching for it, we need a boat, so let's skip this crap and talk money."

"I like him," Captain Richards waggled a finger at the big leader of the mercs. "But sadly, it doesn't matter how much green you throw at me, I can't take you down the river."

"And why is that?" Emma snapped, unable to stop herself.

"That bastard buddy of yours stole my crew," Captain Richards leaned back in his chair, margarita in hand. "Bought them right out from under me."

"What? Why?" Emma demanded.

"When your buddy showed up, there was another boat that happened to be around," Captain Richards told her. "*The Spanish Lady*, captained by a prick named Benji."

"Captain Benjamin," Quin interrupted. "That was his name."

"Right, Benji," Captain Richards went on. "That prick's boat was nicer looking than mine I guess but your guy wasn't content with just getting a nicer boat. McKay wanted experienced rivermen for the crew. That was something Benji didn't have so your man McKay started waving green around and making promises. Before I knew it, my crew was gone and I was stuck here in this village. Not that I am not grateful for you letting me stay, Quin. You know I love you and yours."

"No offense taken, Eli," Quin nodded, "I understand things quite well."

"Couldn't you have just hired another crew if you wanted to leave?" Marcus challenged the captain.

"Sure, mate. . .If I wanted to hire crappy hands and be a bastard like McKay," Captain Richards said. "Not *that* many boats pass through here and most of them are either pirates, college prick woke fraggers looking to save the environment on their way to get eaten by the jungle, or wankers like Benji and his crew."

"How large of a crew do you need to make your boat operational?" Marcus asked.

"Seven or eight I reckon, big man," Captain Richards kept his eyes on Marcus, appraising him. "Let me guess, you've got the people, right?"

"I do," Marcus nodded. "There are fourteen of us counting Dr. Wallace. Among us are an engineer, a communications expert, a medic, and most of us have been on boats before."

Captain Richards couldn't hide the fact that he was getting interested in what Marcus was saying as he countered, "Being on a boat and crewing it are worlds apart."

"We kill folks and blow things up for a living, Captain. I am sure we can manage to learn what's needed," Marcus's bluntness appeared to catch

Captain Richards off guard.

"Okay," Captain Richards shrugged, conceding the argument. "You got a crew for the boat."

"How much then?" Emma asked.

Captain Richards flashed a wry grin. "I think two hundred grand would do it."

"What the hell?" Rachel blurted out. "That's insane!"

Marcus was just irked at the price they had been given.

"Damn," Murphy muttered, "If it weren't for the armor and weapons, I'd guess your boat isn't even worth that much if we were to buy it outright."

"How about we try this again and you offer us a fair price this time?" Marcus growled. "Before you tick me off, son."

"If it was just a sightseeing trip down river, sure, but you and I both know that's not what you're asking of me, is it, mate?" Captain Richards's voice was cold and level.

"Eli is quite correct on that front," Quin chimed in. "This river, especially the paths you seek to take on it, is most dangerous and not just from the pirates. The Ahuizotl prowl the area that your Dr. McKay was headed for. Perhaps they are the reason he has not returned."

"The Ahuio.. What?" Rachel glared at Quin.

"The Ahuizotl," Emma repeated the name.

"They're a race of mythological beings who are supposed to exist in this region."

"Who the frag cares?" Rachel shook her head. "You just said the things are a myth."

"There is often truth in myth," Marcus sighed.

"Oh trust me, my new friends," Quin said, "the Ahuizotl are very real. I have seen them with my own eyes. Though the creatures seldom come this far north but we've had rare encounters with them even here."

"There ya go," Captain Richards smirked. "Hazard pay for myself and my boat. That's what I am asking for. Regardless, the way I see things, my boat is the only ship in the harbor, so to speak."

"One fifty," Emma countered, watching the captain's reaction to it closely.

Captain Richards's attention fell completely on her now. "Two hundred. That's my price."

"We could always just take your boat," Marcus threatened.

"Uh uh," the captain shook his head. "Quin here wouldn't let that happen."

"I am sorry, Mr. Marcus but Eli is right. We will not permit that sort of violence in our home," Quin warned.

Marcus met Quin's eyes. The two stared at each other for a moment. It was Marcus who reluctantly turned his head away first. Emma could see that he enjoyed putting the captain's head on a pike for how he was extorting them but the big man wasn't willing to fight through Quin and his people to do it. They didn't deserve that. A part of Emma wondered if Marcus would go through them if she ordered him to. She wasn't about to find out.

"One seventy five for the use of your boat and skills as its navigator. In addition, you act as our guide once we reach the region we're headed to. You seem to know this area and your way around it. I think that's more than fair," Emma offered.

"I think you must have hit your head or something before dinner, Doctor," Captain Richards snorted. "You just undercut my price and added extra danger for me too."

"You need the money and the crew to get you out of here, Captain," Emma stood her ground. "Accepting my offer is the best thing for both of us."

Captain Richards reached up and took off his red glasses, showing her his green eyes behind them. "You're a pretty good haggler, lady. I'll give you that."

"Does that mean we have a deal then?" Emma pressed him.

"One seventy-five," Captain Richards agreed.

"It's a deal."

****

"The *Hell-bender*?" Emma glanced at Captain Richards as they stood together at the boat's pilot station. "Really?"

"I was born in the American South, Doc. Give a me a break, eh?" He shrugged. "And now that y'all are on her, you got to stop calling me Captain Richards. That was my dad. My name is Eli."

"Okay then, Eli," Emma nodded. "You say you're from the South but you don't always sound like it."

"I could be all lame and claim to be a citizen of the world or some crap like that," Eli chuckled.

"I get it," Emma said.

Eli winked at her. "I am sure you do."

The *Hell-bender* had left the village and its dock behind. She drifted along the river, carried by its current, as Eli steered her. He'd been angry as hell when Emma had told him how early she wanted to get moving. Eli seemed to have forgiven her now but he'd been difficult to deal with during as the sun rose. There were several times he and Marcus had almost gone at each other. Emma had kept them both from doing something they would regret, smoothing things over. Funny thing was that she would have almost paid to see who won that fight. Marcus was a huge man and a hardened merc to boot but Eli, his confidence in dealing with him, suggested that it would be very much a one sided massacre.

It was getting close to noon now and one could easily tell it from the heat. The sun was just as blazing hot as it had been every day since Emma had arrived in South America. For the place to be called a rainforest, she sure hadn't seen a lot of rain yet.

"Your mercs ain't half bad at crewing a boat," Eli smirked.

"I hired the best of the best," Emma assured him.

"You're wasting your time out here. You know that, right?" Eli's smirk had vanished.

"You don't think that the Jewel of the Tlayoalli is real?" Emma frowned.

Eli shrugged. "I've seen a lot of strange things in my time, Doc. Whether the jewel is real or not doesn't matter. I'd lay odds though if we keep the course you've set for us all, none of are going to make it back alive. Tell me, why does this jewel mean so much to you anyway?"

That wasn't an easy question for Emma to answer but she tried. "My father died when I was young."

"Hunting the jewel?" Eli quipped.

"No!" Emma shook her head. "He passed on

from cancer. You going to let me do this or not?"

"Shutting up," Eli made a move to act like he was zipping his lips. Emma thought it was cute and it helped deal with the pain she was feeling at reliving the past.

"I never knew my mother. She died when I was born. My dad was everything to me growing up. When I lost him, it was almost too much to bear. I floundered for a long time but somehow managed to get my grades back on track, got into college, and that's when I met Winston."

"You mean Dr. McKay?" Eli asked.

"Yes," Emma fought not to tear up. "For a time, he was my best friend, my mentor, and a father figure to me. When I got my degree, I stayed on at the university, working for him. He introduced me to the story of the jewel when I was just a student and I joined him in trying to prove it was real and get the funding to go in search of it. The more we learned about it though, the more we drifted apart. Soon, the university decided it could only keep one of us around. McKay threw me under the bus to keep what limited funding there was for our work to himself. And things got worse from there. . ."

Emma's voice had quietly trailed off. Eli was smart enough to leave her alone about it until she could get herself back together.

"Finding that jewel is my life's work, Eli. I'm not going to let that bastard McKay be the one who does it," Emma promised.

"You ever think maybe he did find it and that's why he never came back?" Eli shot her a sideways glance, his hands still holding the boat's wheel.

"If he found it and were still alive to tell about it, you can bet McKay would be shouting to the world about the jewel at the top of his lungs," Emma admitted.

"So really, you're chasing a dead man," Eli pointed out. "I'm just trying to save you and yours a lot of suffering. I wasn't messing with you when I said none of us may make it back. It's bloody fragging dangerous where you're taking us, Doc."

"Why?" Emma looked Eli in the eyes. "Why is it so dangerous, Captain?"

"You believe in this jewel of darkness and its power yet seem to have such a hard time accepting that other dark things are out there in these jungles," Eli sighed.

"You're talking about monsters, aren't you?" Emma rolled her eyes.

"I am," Eli said. "There's crap out there you never want to meet up with. Things that shouldn't exist in the real world but do."

"And you've encountered them before?" Emma wasn't buying any of it.

"Sweetheart, I've killed 'em before," Eli told her. "And I don't ever want to go up against any of them again. . . but where you've got us going, you better believe that's going to happen."

The sound of loud footsteps tore Eli's attention away from her and what they were discussing. Marcus came stomping up to them at the pilot's wheel.

"Just wanted to let you know that your quarters are ready," Marcus said to Emma.

Eli erupted into laughter. "Oh, right! Sometimes I forget that this is your boat and all good sir! How nice of you to prepare them for her. Did you steal the flamethrower out of my quarters too while you were at it?"

Marcus growled. "Watch it, little man."

Then the big man did a double take, "Wait, did you just say you have a flamethrower aboard this boat?"

Then Eli surprised the heck out of her. Emma was taken aback as he suddenly backed down with his attitude.

"Look, Marcus, I get it," Eli said. "You needed to check them out for her. It's your job, mate. Guess we should all start thinking like we're on the same team now because we are. The doc here is boss of us both."

Marcus was just as shocked as Emma was. He

gave Eli a respectful nod. "So how are we progressing with getting to where we're headed?"

"Ha," Eli grinned, "I'd answer that if I knew exactly where we were heading. Right now, we're just cruising southward. She hasn't told me to do anything else yet."

Marcus's eyes cut towards Emma.

"Did you get out the gear I asked for?" Emma asked the big man.

"Yep," Marcus answered. "It's set up on the main deck toward the bow as you asked."

"Well then, Captain," it was Emma's turn to give a wry grin, "I'll be letting you know more on exactly where we're headed within the hour."

Emma left Eli and Marcus, walking down to the main deck.

Eli watched as she went straight to the large metal box Marcus had brought out for her. With the touch of her fingerprint to its security lock, the box opened. Within it, was some Sci-Fi looking gadget thingy that made Eli smirk again. Emma fidgeted with the device. Eli figured she was adjusting it.

"What is that thing?" Eli asked Marcus.

"Hell if I know," the big merc grunted. "She said it tracks certain kinds of energy emissions or some crap like that. Dr. Wallace thinks she'll be able to track the jewel she's after with it."

"You really think that thing will work?" Eli sounded skeptical.

"I've got faith in her not the machine," Marcus said firmly. "If that jewel is out there, she'll find it."

****

Night fell over the Amazon, engulfing its banks in shadow. Rachel had thought it was loud during the day but that was nothing compared to the noises ringing out from the dark jungle. The noises during the day, though loud, could have been called peaceful, at least to a degree. Now, it was as if everything was waking up, a storm of nature coming alive. The noises ranged from the buzzing of millions of insects to the shifting of the brush as small animals moved through. Every so often a piercing cry or inhuman shriek would pierce the black of darkness. The first few had startled both her and Froggy who was on watch with her. The portly soldier's face was pale in the moonlight. Really it was more pink than white at this point. Froggy was sunburnt. She could see that even through his dense, red beard. Rachel saw her own tenseness in him. Everyone in the unit was dealing with the oddness of this gig in different ways. Some by not dealing with it at all. Rachel had a bad feeling that things weren't going to go their way and couldn't seem to shake it no matter what she did. It almost made her wish that she was a smoker just to have something to take the edge off.

Froggy must have noticed her expression because he said, "It's spooky out here, isn't it, ma'am?"

He and Rachel were positioned at the *Hell-bender's* bow. Nadja and Chris were in matching positions at the stern. Haus had volunteered to take over for Captain Richards overnight. The burly veteran had experience with river boats and had been the perfect choice for the job. It hadn't been easy for Marcus to convince the captain of that though. Aside from the five of them, everyone else was below deck either in their quarters Captain Richards had given them or sleeping in the *Hell-bender's* nearly empty hold. She was a cargo ship so there was plenty of space for those who didn't rate quarters to bunk down in their sleeping bags. Rachel slapped at a mosquito biting the side of her neck and grimaced as she looked at its squished corpse on the palm of her hand.

"That's one way to put it," Rachel huffed. "This place. . ."

"It's nothing like the Sandbox," Froggy snorted. "I'll give it that."

Rachel didn't respond to his comment. She'd

lost a lot of friends in the Middle East. Her eyes scanned the shoreline for any signs of trouble, half expecting to see the painted faces of indigenous cannibals amid the trees and brush, blowguns and bows aimed at them.

"Hey," Froggy said, getting up from where he sat, moving closer to her, with his cell phone in his hand. Its screen glowed green in the dim light of the moon and stars. "Check this out."

"Don't tell me you've got signal out here," Rachel gawked at the portly redhead.

"Hell no," Froggy shook his head. "That'd be impossible. But that village, they had some kind of satellite Wi-Fi or something. I was able to get online there. Anyway, Murphy told me about these creatures that are supposed to live in these parts. Take a look at this."

Froggy thrust his phone at her. Sighing, Rachel looked at its screen. She had no idea what the frag the thing on it was supposed to be. The creature was like some kind of bizarre, twisted dog with both hair and scales. Rachel blinked as she noticed its front paws weren't paws at all, they were basically human hands only it had fingers tipped with long, deadly looking nails. Whatever the thing was, it was snarling in the image, showing off the gleaming, razor teeth inside its mouth. Something about the odd mixture made her think of primates. There was a frightening intelligence in the creature's glowing white eyes. Its tail rose high above the creature's body, arced like a scorpion's but instead of ending in a stinger, the tail ended with what appeared to be large, human hand. Rachel shivered though the air around her was still muggy and hot. Not even the fall of night had chased the heat of the day away, not entirely.

Rachel pulled away from the phone not wanting to see the image on its screen anymore. "Get that thing out of my face, Froggy."

He chuckled, taking another glance at the screen himself. "Ah, it's not that bad. Besides, crap like that isn't real. We've both been through the grinder enough to know the only monsters in this world are us."

"What's that thing called?" Rachel asked and instantly regretted doing so.

"It's called an Ahuizotl," the excitement in Froggy's voice hammered into her almost like a physical force. "That translates to something water dog according to my web search. It's not just a single creature! There are bunches of them. In some myths, they're servants of the gods who take the souls of good people that on to heaven. In others, the things are just monsters that like to kill people. The only thing I could find that is a constant throughout all the stories about them is that they hunt humans."

"That's great, Froggy," Rachel stared at him. "Now, why don't you sit back down, shut up, and do your job? We're on watch, aren't we?"

If Froggy was offended by her rudeness, he didn't show it. Most were used to her rather gruff manners.

"Yes, ma'am," Froggy said and did as she had ordered.

Rachel caught sight of something moving in the water in the corner of her eye. She jerked around, looking out over the port side of the boat.

"What is it?" Froggy demanded too loudly for Rachel's liking, leaping to his feet, weapon at the ready. Like herself, the portly redhead was packing an M-4 carbine. While their unit had no standard issue weapon, the M-4 was common among them.

"Keep your voice down, damn it," Rachel hissed.

Froggy shut up, staring at her, waiting for an answer to his question.

"I didn't get a good look," Rachel whispered. "Could be nothing."

"Or it could be a cannibal with a knife in his mouth creeping up on us in the dark," Froggy countered.

Rachel ignored Froggy, keeping her focus on the water, watching its surface closely. She wondered exactly what she had seen. Surely, it was nothing more than just a croc or gator. Rachel didn't know for sure that either crocs or gators were native to the region but it seemed like one always saw them in movies when people were on river boats like the *Hell-bender.*

"Should we be sounding an alarm?" Froggy whispered.

"What the hell for?" Rachel asked. "I don't see anything anymore, do you?"

Froggy shook his head, glaring at her. She was the one who had stirred things up in the first place.

Doubting herself and blaming everything on her nerves, Rachel took a deep breath.

Seeing her do so, Froggy relaxed too. Neither one of them was expecting anything when the attack came. Water splashed as the snake broke the surface of the river, striking at Froggy from behind. Its massive head shot over the side of the *Hell-bender's* deck, mouth open. Dagger-like teeth sunk into Froggy as he howled in pain. The snake pulled the portly soldier over the side. Rachel lost sight of them. She rushed to the railing that Froggy had just been yanked over, eyes scanning the river for any sign of Froggy or the snake.

Haus must have seen what happened from the

pilot wheel. He came running up to her.

"What the hell just happened?" he asked.

Both of them heard footsteps racing up from behind them. They belonged to Nadja. She must have left Chris at the *Hell-bender's* stern because the tech wasn't with her.

"It was a snake," Rachel told Haus. "A fragging, big mother of a snake."

Nadja skidded to a halt, looking at them. She cocked her head to one side as if hearing something in the night that they couldn't.

"Watch it!" Nadja yelled as the snake exploded upwards out of the river again. Its head was roughly the size of a large dog's torso, shooting straight for Nadja. The woman's hands moved like lightning. Her hatchets slashed out cutting a bloody swath of torn scales, sending bright red blood flying as they impacted with the giant snake's head. Despite the damage they did, it wasn't enough to stop the snake from finishing its strike. The thing's jaws closed around Nadja's upper right leg with the sharp cracking sound of breaking bone. Nadja cried out in pain but didn't let loose of her hatchets. As the snake swept her from the deck, her body dangling beneath its massive head, Nadja struck at it again. The blades of her weapons sunk into the snake's flesh only to be ripped free and hammered there again. More blood flew, splattering over Nadja.

"I don't have a shot!" Haus shouted. The burly man didn't have his trademark mini-gun with him but had drawn his sidearm, its barrel pointed towards the snake where it slung Nadja about above the ship's bow.

Nadja wailed as her leg tore loose from her torso. The red-slicked white of her femur gleamed in the moonlight, protruding from the edge of the snake's mouth. The rest of her thudded onto the *Hell-bender's* deck with enough force to dislocate her left shoulder and crack several of her ribs inside her chest. The hatchets went bouncing away from Nadja's broken body as the impact knocked them from her grasp.

As the snake dove back for the water, its prize clutched within its mouth, Rachel opened fire with her M-4. Bullets punched through scale but without the power to stop the giant snake. It splashed into the water, vanishing from her sight.

This time, the thing didn't remain there. It came right back up, striking at her with burning rage in its eyes. As soon as its body was above the level of the deck, the night was lit up by the *Hell-bender's* forward .50 caliber roaring to life. Orange tracers burnt in the darkness as the high-power rounds sliced the snake's body in half. Both the severed upper portion and the jagged, bloody stump of its lower body flopped into the river. Rachel looked around to see Captain Eli Richards with his hands on the fifty caliber's firing mechanisms.

"Guess I should have warned you about those, huh?" Captain Richards frowned. "Those things can be real bastards if they get the drop on you."

****

"What the fragging hell?" Marcus raged, slamming a fist down on top of the table in the small room where he, the captain, Dr. Wallace, Rachel, and Murphy were meeting. "I've got two people dead!"

"Crap happens out here, big guy," Captain Eli Richards was leaning back in his chair. "I'm sorry. . ."

"You're fragging sorry?" Marcus snapped.

"That's enough, Marcus!" Emma shouted.

"Look, y'all knew how dangerous it is on this river before you came here," Eli told them all.

Marcus grunted but said nothing more.

"What the hell was that thing?" Murphy asked.

Eli gave him a wry look. "Seriously? It was a snake, man."

"I've never seen anything like that thing in my life before," Murphy said.

"I haven't either," Emma kept her eyes on Marcus, hoping the big guy didn't do anything they'd all regret. "But I have heard of them. There are plenty of stories about giant snakes like that in this region."

It was clear by his expression that Marcus had never given stories like what she was talking about much credence. . .until now.

"Things like this happen," Eli assured them. "I've lost crew to snakes like that one before. All you can do is just be careful, keep an eye out, and hope for the best; even then sometimes. . ."

"You should have warned us," Marcus pressed Eli.

"You're a group of battle hardened mercs, armed to the teeth, and sure as hell seemed to know what you were doing," Eli shot back. "Even if I had specifically told you about the snakes out here, what could you have done differently? You were already smart enough to have two people on watch at a time and pairs at each end of the boat."

"Our goal is still the same," Emma said calmy. "I am sorry for your loss, Marcus, but you know this doesn't change anything."

"I am well aware of what my job is, Dr. Wallace," Marcus scowled. "I don't need to be reminded of it."

"Good." Emma felt bad for the loss of Marcus's people but it was their job. They all knew the risks of their occupation and what the cost of earning their next paycheck might be.

"Are there other things out there that we need to be aware of, Captain?" Marcus snarled.

"Mate, just about everything out here wants you dead," Eli met the big man's eyes. "You're professionals. Deal with it."

"We're more aware of the danger now, Marcus," Emma said. "What can we do to keep this from happening again?"

"More people on watch will be a good start," Marcus shrugged. "And from now on, this boat's weapons are going to be manned and ready for action."

"I'm good with that," Eli smiled. "That's fine with me."

"I didn't ask," Marcus said.

"Whatever," Eli didn't rise to Marcus trying to push him into an angry response.

Marcus huffed and stormed out. Murphy, looking uncomfortable, followed after the big man.

Emma let him go. The others needed to be updated on the changes they had decided on anyway. She looked over at Eli. Rationally, Emma knew he wasn't to blame for the deaths that happened tonight. Marcus and his people should be able to handle things better from here on out now that they were aware that this place. . . well, it was as deadly as it was wet and there were *things* in the jungle that were more than just stories.

"Emma. . ." Eli began but she held up a hand, stopping him.

"I don't want to hear it, Eli," she told him. "What's done is done. Let's just make sure that we don't lose anyone else."

She could see he was trying hard not to tell her that he had told her this would happen.

"We've got a long ways to go yet," Eli finally said.

"Not as far as you may think," Emma frowned.

Eli leaned across the table. "I take it your machine picked up something this afternoon?"

Emma nodded. "I have an exact fix on the location of the jewel."

"Something like that would be nice to have been told," Eli griped.

"Your current course was in line with where we needed to go. There was no reason to tell you anything yet," Emma smirked. "Remember, Captain, you work for me."

"Yeah, but this is still my boat," Eli shook his head and got up. He walked over to a desk in the corner of the room, picking up a rolled up paper, and came back to the table. As Eli was unrolling it across the table top, Emma saw that the paper was a map.

"I didn't think there were any real maps of this

region," Emma commented.

Eli shrugged. "There aren't. Not really. This is something I've put together myself over time from my experiences here."

"I see," Emma was impressed. In that moment, Eli made her think of the boat captains of the old world. He was certainly just as brave and adventurous.

"Show me where," Eli said.

Emma studied his hand-drawn map, examining it closely. "Where are we now?"

He showed her.

She thought things over and then put a finger on the map. "The jewel has to be around there from the readings I got."

Eli's expression grew dark. "Are you sure?"

"Ninety-nine percent," Emma answered. "The amount of energy coming out of that place couldn't be anything else. Why are you looking at the map like that?"

"That's a bad place," Eli told her.

"You've been there?" Emma asked, shocked.

Eli shook his head. "Nope. I know of it though. The folks who live in the jungle call it the City of Death. Kind of cliché', I reckon, but a fitting name. No one I know has ever been there and come back to tell about the place."

"That's so lame," Emma frowned. "It sounds

like a really badly written horror movie."

Eli smiled. "It does, doesn't it?"

He dug out a cigarette and lit up. "The place is dangerous as hell though. There ain't no denying that. I wasn't kidding when I said no one ever came back from it. The native folk won't go anywhere near it."

"Any idea what's there?" Emma asked.

"Evil? Monsters? Vampire chickens? Whatever the hell is there isn't something you want to mess with," Eli assured her despite slipping in a joke.

"I got that," Emma sighed and then grinned at the eccentric river boat captain. "Vampire chickens? Really?"

"Like I said, I am from the South," Eli laughed, further easing the tension they were both feeling. "Lots of crazy things in those backwoods."

"I bet," Emma chuckled before looking at the map again. "So how much longer do you think it'll take us to get there?"

Eli tapped the map, "If that's really where we're going, I'd guess another night, maybe two on the river depending on the current and how careful we want to be in regards to fuel. Then maybe we've got another day or so hoofing it on foot through the jungle."

"We?" Emma was surprised by his choice of

words. "You make it sound like you'll be joining us in the jungle, Eli. The way I see things, your job ends at the river bank when we can't go any further on the water."

"You'd think that wouldn't you, eh?" Eli grinned. "But there's no way I am letting you and your gang go into that jungle without a guide."

"I thought you said you'd never been there," Emma pointed out.

"I haven't but I know the jungle. You and your people don't. Walking in there even more blind than you folk already are is like asking to get torn apart by the first batch of hungry things you stumble across."

"Things?" Emma asked.

"Things," Eli nodded. "We've covered that part."

"I guess we have," Emma agreed.

****

Marcus paced the forward deck of the *Hellbender*. The night had been just that. . . hell. Losing people was part of the gig but two already? That stung Marcus. The guilt of it weighed on him heavily. He should have been more on guard, more believing of the crap that apparently existed on and in this blasted river. His jaws worked, chomping on the gum in his mouth, his teeth grinding it.

Alex and Olivia were on watch not far from him. Alex was manning the fifty caliber, keeping an eye on the river bank while Olivia was sitting next to him, her eyes watching the river itself. There was a heavy air of defeat that hung over his entire crew almost as if it were a tangible force. The loss of Froggy had hit them all hard. The portly redhead had brought a jolliness that would surely be missed to their ranks. Marcus still could barely believe he was gone. . . but at least Froggy's death had been quick. Nadja had held on for hours, suffering, bleeding out from her wounds, and in pain from her shattered bones. Tali had done all she could for Nadja with her limited resources. Everyone knew she had. No one put any blame on the medic. And Nadja . . . a badass to the end, refused to be so doped up on morphine that she'd be out when she passed. Nadja died with her eyes open, fighting, just like she'd done throughout the rest of her life. Watching her had been one of the most painful experiences of Marcus's life.

After Nadja had passed, Marcus hadn't been able to sleep. He'd collected her hatchets, cleaned them, and added them to his own weapons. It was nearing noon. The sun was still climbing towards its zenith in the sky above. The toll of the night was catching up to him but Marcus knew it would be pointless to try to get some rest yet. His mind was churning. He headed into the *Hell-bender's* interior, below the main deck to the boat's small kitchen area to find Rachel sitting at the table there. Her eyes were bloodshot and she looked as tired as he felt.

"Couldn't sleep either, huh?" Marcus moved to pour himself a cup of coffee. It smelled freshly made and he was sure Rachel was to thank for that.

"Not a wink," Rachel answered, taking a sip from the mug in her hand.

"It's all sort of surreal, isn't it?" Marcus asked.

"What?" Rachel glanced up at him as he slid out a chair and sat down across from her.

"This job," Marcus grunted.

"Giant snakes are certainly something new to contend with. Can't blame yourself for what happened, you know? No one could have seen that coming," Rachel managed a weak smile.

"Who says I am blaming myself?" Marcus challenged her.

"Don't give me that crap, boss," Rachel shifted in her chair. "I've worked with you long enough to know how you think."

Marcus cocked an eyebrow. "I suppose that's true. Still. . ."

"Still, you gotta stop," Rachel cut him off. "Your focus. . .our focus. . .needs to stay on what's ahead. We've got to keep our heads in the game, not be emotional, or we're all likely dead already."

"Likely?" Marcus snorted, giving her back some grief of his own.

Rachel smiled.

"Thanks for the coffee," Marcus waved his mug at her.

"No problem, boss," Rachel nodded and then changed the subject. "That snake sure shook us all up."

"God only knows what we'll be up against in the jungle," Marcus sighed.

"Not Bigfoot at least," Rachel chuckled.

Marcus shook his head fondly at her. "Remind me why I hired you?"

"Because I am a pro and I get things done," Rachel told him firmly.

"I can't argue you that," Marcus grinned.

"You better not," Rachel warned him. "And let me tell you, we're sure as hell going to feel Froggy's loss on this gig."

"I know," Marcus agreed. Froggy had been their comm. expert. They still had his gear and sat phone but if anything went wrong with them, they were screwed. Calling out for help had never been the plan but knowing for sure that they had the option to try would have been good.

"Sucks about Nadja too. She was one hell of a

fighter," Rachel commented.

Marcus finished his coffee and got up. He could feel Rachel's eyes on him, checking out the hatchets strapped to his thighs.

"Try to get some rest," Marcus told her. "That's an order, Rachel."

"Yes sir," she nodded at him.

Marcus left her venturing back out onto the main deck. The heat and mugginess of the day was horrible. Marcus's hand slapped through the air near his face trying to drive away a mosquito. The bugs on the river were relentless and seemed limitless in number.

There was no sign of Dr. Wallace or the captain. Haus had shown himself though. The burly man was standing, staring out at the river banks, over the *Hell-bender's* port side railing. Marcus walked over to join him there.

"Gonna be bad, sir," Haus said without even glancing in his direction. "Maybe we should let this one go and turn around while we still can."

Marcus blinked in surprise. A statement like that from Haus was enough to shake Marcus to his core. The grizzled veteran wasn't the sort of man who said things like that lightly or without reason.

"We can't turn around, Haus," Marcus reminded him. "We need this gig as much as Dr. Wallace needs us."

"Just saying, I got a bad feeling about this one, sir," Haus's deep voice rumbled. "Money ain't everything."

"This gig is what's keeping the company afloat right now," Marcus sighed. "We screw this up and. . ."

"And we'll get another job like always," Haus grunted. "There are plenty enough folks out there looking to hire killers and muscle men like us."

"That's true I suppose, Haus, but we made a commitment to Dr. Wallace and we are going to honor it. Failing to would damage our rep. Maybe beyond repair in some circles," Marcus pointed out. "We are in this whether we like it or not."

"Then I guess you better get ready for the guilt of more death on you," Haus huffed and left his place at the railing, heading back towards the entrance to the *Hell-bender's* interior.

Marcus let the sour, burly man go. Haus had spoken his mind and was done with their talk. There was nothing more for either of them to say anyway. Marcus knew he wasn't going to change Haus's mind about how things were going to go. Hell, Marcus figured the grizzled veteran was right but he was dang sure planning on trying to prove him wrong.

****

As night fell over the river on the second night

of the *Hell-bender's* southward journey, things were very different on her deck. Marcus's crew had set up additional lights that illuminated the bulk of her from one end to the other, leaving only rare, scattered areas of shadow. Instead of four people on watch with two at the bow and two at the stern, there was now an additional two mercs patrolling around the length of the boat. Haus was at the boat's wheel again, high above and behind the bow, looking down on it.

Chad and Dan were the two mercs on patrol. Their routes and pace kept them on opposite sides of the *Hell-bender*. Chad didn't care for being alone as he walked along the port side of the boat. He hated snakes. Who didn't? The things spooked him. He would much rather face an entire squad of killers in the Sandbox alone than a thing like the one that had attacked them the night before. Everyone had gotten a look at the giant creature's corpse in the aftermath of the battle that had cost Froggy and Nadja their lives. There was so much of the thing's blood in the water that the entire river around the boat seemed to have been turned red. The worst part of it for Chad though was seeing the giant snake's head, its jaws opening and closing in death. Just the thought of it made him shiver despite the warm humidity of the night air. Chad shook his head, chasing away the image of the giant snake's mouth.

He came to a stop alongside the halfway point of the *Hell-bender's* wheelhouse. Chad knew that Haus was up there somewhere above him, steering the boat through the darkness. So far, the night had been quiet with no sign of trouble.

A soft splashing noise came from the water below. Chad stepped over to the railing, looking downward. He couldn't see anything but the movement of the river water. Relaxing a bit, Chad kept his position at the railing but turned his eyes upwards towards the distant shore bank. There was nothing noticeable to be seen there either.

"Just a fish or something," Chad muttered to himself.

His nerves were like frayed wires and he was aware of it, his fear of snakes amping up his anxiety. Trying to get his head back in the game, Chad focused on his weapon, giving it a quick check over. His M-4 was good though it didn't bring him a lot of comfort. The rifle wouldn't do much if another snake like the one from last night came at him; the creature would be far too large to be easily stopped.

Behind Chad, an elongated arm rose up over the *Hell-bender's* side railing. The hand closed around his neck before Chad ever noticed it was near him, super strong fingers tightening to stop any screams. Two more hands reached around his body, taking hold of his rifle with blinding speed, roughly removing it from his grasp. The weapon clattered to the deck at Chad's feet as the hands that had disarmed him grabbed his arms, pinning them to his sides. Chad struggled against the arms holding him but they were superhumanly strong and held him tight. He tried to ram his head backwards in hope of hitting his attacker but couldn't move it at all. The hand around his neck had a steel grip on him. Chad couldn't breathe. His struggling grew weaker and weaker. Vision blurring, Chad made a final effort to try and flip his attack over him but that failed as well. The attacker's body just shifted with his own.

Finally, Chad couldn't take any more. The world before his eyes went black and his body went limp in the arms of his attacker. Chad was unconscious as the creature holding him lowered his corpse onto the deck. There hadn't been enough noise to draw the attention of Haus where the burly veteran was at the boat's wheel above. The sounds of the jungle and the current of the river had masked the quiet noises of the struggle.

Dan was walking along, on patrol, puffing on a smoke and wishing the night was cooler. Like most everyone on Marcus's crew, he'd had enough of the jungle's oppressive humidity. He sure as hell wasn't prepared to see Chad lying on the deck with a strange creature kneeling over him as he came around the corner of the wheelhouse. The thing was a bit smaller than a man. Its body was covered in wet, spiky fur that was midnight black. The thing was a sick cross between a dog and monkey. A long tail extended above it like that of a scorpion's only instead of ending in a stringer, there was an overly large, human-like hand, fingers tipped with gleaming, sharp nails. Around its head was a mane of white hair as the creature rose up from where it knelt, turning its head towards him. The thing's eyes were a burning red that glowed in the shadows beneath the wheelhouse. Dan, shocked and hands trembling, jerked up his rifle, but couldn't risk taking a shot at the creature because of how close it was to Chad. He thought the monstrous thing was going to lunge at him but it didn't. Whatever the hell it was, the thing jumped up and over the boat's side railing, plunging into the river with a loud splash.

****

Emma stood on the deck of the *Hell-bender* with Tali, Marcus, Rachel, and Eli. Dan was with them but the man was out of it. He sat, back against the side of the wheelhouse, rocking back and forth, muttering about not being able to save Chad, whose corpse lay sprawled out in a puddle of his own blood. It slicked the deck red. Dan had managed to tell them that a monster had been responsible for killing Chad but he hadn't been able to describe it much.

"What. . .what did it do him?" Emma asked.

Tali was examining Chad. "There are finger marks on his neck. Whatever killed him choked Chad to death and must have caught him so off guard that he didn't even have time to scream."

"You're right about that," Marcus grunted. "If he had, someone would have heard him and come running."

"But it didn't stop at just killing him," Tali said pointing at the gaping holes of jagged, torn flesh where Chad's eyes had been. "The thing took his eyes. Ripped them right out of their sockets. As weird as that is, it gets weirder. Some of his teeth have been torn from his mouth and all of his fingernails are missing."

"That is seriously messed up." Rachel pressed the side of a clenched fist to her lips, fighting off the urge to vomit.

"No, it's not," Eli cut in. "What killed your friend there was an Ahuizotl. Some folks call them water dogs. And the parts that are missing from your man are the exact parts they're known for taking from their victims."

"Here we go again," Marcus sighed. "More

myths come to life."

"The proof is right there in front of you, man," Eli gestured at Chad's corpse. "And I'll tell you this, where there is one Ahuizotl, you can bet there are a bunch of the things. I've run into them several times before out here. The good news is that they're a hell of a lot easier to kill than that giant snake was."

"How the hell did it get on the boat without being noticed?" Marcus demanded of Eli.

"The things are slippery bastards, mate," Eli frowned. "They're masters of stealth, like little canine ninjas."

"We can't leave Chad's body here," Tali said. "It needs to be disposed of like Nadja's."

They'd been forced to just toss hers into the river and Marcus knew they were going to have to do the same with Chad. That really ticked him off. His crew were good people and deserved better but there wasn't a blasted thing he could do about it. Even his extra precautions with increasing the night watch hadn't saved Chad's life. Now the man was going to be dumped into the river like garbage.

Rachel, apparently sensing his distress, stepped up to Marcus, putting a hand on his shoulder. "I'll see that it gets done, sir."

Marcus nodded, following Emma and Eli as

they headed up to the top of the wheelhouse.

Tali remained behind with Rachel not only to help dispose of Chad's corpse but to see what she could do for Dan.

"Hey!" Marcus called after Eli.

The captain turned around to face him as they neared the boat's wheel where Haus stood.

"Are you sure about there being more of those things in the river?" Marcus demanded.

"Did I sound like I wasn't?" Eli frowned.

"You ran into them before. How did you deal with the things?" Marcus didn't care for asking Eli for advice but given the circumstances. . .

"Just like you have," Eli answered. "I doubled the watch and lit up as much of the deck as I could but I still lost people. Like I said before we ever left the village, it's dangerous out here. Just about everything wants to kill you and eat you."

Marcus was frustrated as hell. The big man growled, "And you just accepted the loss as part of your job?"

"Don't you?" Eli countered.

Having no answer to that he wanted to say aloud, Marcus turned to Emma. "We'll come up with a better plan. I'm not losing anyone else."

Emma nodded, not knowing what the big man expected her to say. She wasn't heartless but at the same time, what mattered to her was finding the jewel. Marcus and his crew were being paid to take the risks they were in order to protect her.

The three of them reached the top of the wheelhouse where Haus stood as a cacophony of horrid cries rang out in the night.

"What the hell is that?" Haus asked.

"Hell is exactly what it is," Eli mumbled, going pale. He roughly shoved Haus out of the way, grabbing hold of the *Hell-bender's* wheel. "Get to the engine room and give me all the power you can."

Haus looked at Marcus.

"You heard him! Go!" Marcus ordered.

Haus took off running without looking back.

"We're screwed if we don't get out of here fast," Eli warned, waiting for Haus to fire up the engine.

"What do you mean?" Marcus spat. "What are those cries?"

"It's not just one Ahuizotl out there," Eli answered. "There's an entire fragging pack of the things!"

Eli worked the throttle next to the *Hell-bender's* wheel. The boat surged forward in the water. It was a lot closer to the shore on the port side than Eli liked. The engine roared loudly, building up power.

The radio on Marcus's belt squawked. The big man grabbed it off his belt as Haus's voice came over it.

"There's one of those things in here!" Haus shouted and then the radio went silent other than the sound of crackling static. At the same time, the *Hell-bender's* main power went offline, her engine sputtering and dying.

"Frag it!" Eli yelled, smashing a fist into the boat's wheel.

Marcus hit the broadcast button on his radio. "Everyone on deck, if something moves that's not one of us, shoot the hell out of it!"

"Holy. . .!" Alex screamed at his position manning the *Hell-bender's* rear fifty cal. He was pointing at the shore.

Dozens of water dogs came crashing out of the brush, their hair spikey, eyes burning red, and snarling with rage and hunger. One of the things leapt into the air, grabbing hold of a low hanging tree limb with the hand that topped its long tail. Using its momentum, the creature catapulted itself through the night to land on the side of the *Hell-Bender.* The creature came scrambling up over the railing onto the deck as both of the boat's fifty calibers opened up on the rest of the charging water dogs. One of the Ahuizotls was literally ripped to pieces as a stream of fifty cal. rounds struck it. Several others lost legs or had their tails blown off of their bodies. The creatures were fast though and very quickly escaped the kill zone of the *Hell-bender's* deck guns, splashing into the water of the river and vanishing beneath its surface.

The Ahuizotl that had boarded the boat found itself face to face with Tali and Dan. The medic was helping steady Dan, trying to get the delusional soldier somewhere safer than the open deck. Tali let out a startled scream, loosing her grip on Dan. His muttering and mumblings stopped as Dan flew into a berserker rage, hurling himself at the monster. The water dog slashed at him with the claws of its tail hand. They dug deep across Dan's chest, tearing through his shirt and flesh. The attack didn't even slow Dan down however, the man was too consumed by his desire to kill the water dog. Dan grabbed the Ahuizotl by its neck as the water dog rose up to meet him. There was a loud cracking noise as Dan wrested the creature's head hard to the left with both his hands. Its body went limp as Dan lifted the water dog up from the deck and managed to lob it over the railing. The water dog's corpse splashed into the river below. Only then did Dan cry out in pain, staggering, and clutching at the mangled mess of his chest.

Tali couldn't believe what she had just seen. It took her a second to recover before she ran to Dan where he had finally collapsed. The wounds on his chest were bad. The medic dropped to her knees, trying to dig out something to stop the bleeding out of her pack.

"We can't let them get on the boat!" Eli warned Marcus. "We won't stand a chance against that many of them in close quarters."

Eli drew the pistols holstered on his hips with the speed of an Old West gunfighter, bounding away from the *Hell-bender's* wheel.

"Emma! Keep her away from the shore!" Eli shouted back at the doctor as he sprinted to join the firing line forming along the *Hell-bender's* port side.

There were water dogs all over that side of the boat now, coming up out the river, scampering up its hull toward the deck. M-4s roared and shotguns boomed, sending water dogs to hell. Tali drew her pistol, getting to her feet, as another water dog came leaping up over the railing. It landed on the deck only a few feet from her, lips parted in a feral snarl. Before Tali could even bring her pistol to bear on the creature though its head burst apart in a shower of exploding bone fragments, blood, and brain matter. Tali looked over the thing's headless corpse to see Brian smiling at her.

"Look out!" Tali shouted as another water dog

appeared, clinging to the railing, and trying to heave itself up and over it.

Brian worked the pump of his shotgun chambering a fresh round as he spun around to face the new threat. His shotgun thundered again, blowing a gaping hole through the monster's body at point blank range. The water dog's hand like hands released the railing and toppled backwards away from the *Hell-bender*. Brian worked the pump again before firing off another round at a water dog that leaped onto the deck a few yards from his position. The blast caught the water dog in its side. An explosion of gore and guts splattered outward as the heavy shotgun slug punched inward. The creature was flung over by the force of the impact. It lay twitching on the deck, innards leaking out.

"Let's move!" Brian yelled at Tali, waving for the medic to catch up with him as he ran for the *Hell-bender's* stern.

The entire deck of the boat was nothing but chaos now. Despite all the water dogs that had been blown apart on the shore and in the water, the things just kept coming. Captain Eli Richards jumped over the railing of the stairs leading down from the wheelhouse, landing gracefully on the deck, pistols in his hands. His right pistol fired first, then his left, as Eli sent a water dog to hell, putting a bullet in each of the monster's eyes. He moved with uncanny speed, engaging a second creature in his path. His pistols rang out in a chorus of shots that hammered into the water dog's chest as the thing tried to stand up right. The water dog's corpse flopped head over heels backwards into the river. Eli had already engaged a third creature before the second's body even landed in the water. Emma watched him, amazed that any human could move like he was. The man was like a force of nature.

Marcus grunted as a water dog rammed into him. He held the creature's clawed hands at bay with his M4, the rifle turned sideways, each of them grasping it. The water dog's tail hand snapped towards his face like a striking snake. Marcus twisted his head trying to avoid the hand but it still struck him a glancing blow. The attack didn't cause the big man to be thrown off as the creature had likely hoped, instead it filled him with fresh rage. Marcus let go of his M4. The water dog, wide eyed and still clutching the rifle, tumbled forward into his arms. The big man caught the creature, lifting it up over his head, and then brought it down over his knee. The water dog's spine snapped with a sharp cracking noise. Marcus tossed its broken body away, snatching up his weapon. He braced the rifle against his shoulder, taking aim at another of the water dogs bounding towards Emma. Squeezing the trigger, he met the charging water dog with a stream of fully automatic rounds that tore into the creature's head and shoulders. The monster died, wailing, collapsing only to keep sliding on across the deck towards the doctor, carried on by its own earlier momentum.

Alex had to abandon his position at the *Hellbender's* forward fifty caliber as the deck around him was swarmed by water dogs. Where all the things had come from, he had no idea. Some had made it through the kill zone coming from the shore but most seemed to be rising up out of the river itself. He blasted one with a burst from his M4 then swung the weapon around to the right, taking a shot at another. Alex didn't see the water dog coming up on him from behind. The creature plowed into him, knocking him over onto the deck. He lost his grip on his M4 and the rifle went bouncing away from him. Alex rolled over to try to fight off the water dog as the thing growled above him. Its growl was a like a chorus of voices in one, demonic and utterly unnatural. He threw an arm up in between his neck and the water dog's mouth. Razor-sharp teeth sunk into his flesh. His own blood splattered into his eyes from the bite as the water dog shook its head, teeth still buried in his arm, tearing it up more. Cursing, Alex ripped his arm out of the monster's mouth as his other arm swung up. The clenched fist of his uninjured arm slammed into the water dog's head. The water dog was knocked off of him. Alex rolled with the creature, trading positions with it so that he was now the one on top. His plan had been to draw the pistol on his hip and blow out the water dog's brains with a point blank shot as he held it down. Things didn't go that way however. The water dog was far faster than Alex had anticipated. Its head came up, attacking him again. Alex screamed in pain and horror as the thing's teeth tore away his manhood. Clutching the red mess of his groin, Alex fell sideways, thudding onto the deck. The water dog was on him again in a fraction of a second, finishing him by tearing out the soft flesh of his lower throat.

Rachel swung the butt of her M4 like a baseball bat. It thudded into the head of a water dog with the sickening sound of crunching skull bone. The water dog, one eye popped loose from its socket, was knocked from her path. Rachel kept on the move, flipping her rifle around in her hands, popping the weapon's spent magazine. She rammed a fresh magazine home, running for the steps that led up to the top of the wheelhouse. They needed some kind of tactical advantage, something to turn the tide of the battle fast or they were all going to be dead meat. Rachel had a plan. Even she was willing to admit it wasn't a genius one but. . . one made do.

Emma was holding the *Hell-bender's* wheel and doing her best to steer farther away from the shore. They were just drifting with the river's current now as the engine was dead. Marcus was keeping the water dogs away from Emma and the wheel. The big man had lost his rifle. In his hands was a piece of metal railing he'd wrested free that he was using like a makeshift spear. A water dog jumped at him but the tip of his spear rose up to meet it, impaling the beast. Marcus shifted his stance using the water dog's own weight to fling it aside and free of his weapon.

Below the battle raging on the *Hell-bender's* deck another struggle was being fought. Haus sucked in air, backpedaled from the red-eyed beast blocking his path to the boat's engine. His upper body was covered with the slash marks from the thing's claws. Blood flowed freely from them, running down the curves of his burly body. The water dog was just as messed up. Where the hand atop its tail should have been, there was nothing but a bloody stump. One of its back legs was broken, the white of shattered bone protruding through punctured flesh. Both of them had given the other hell. Haus could hear the sounds of the battle on the deck above and knew he needed to get the power back on as soon as possible.

"Come on, you mother," Haus challenged the water dog, daring it to come at him again.

The Ahuizotl was keeping its distance from him. He'd hurt it badly but not enough to get the creature to give up yet. Keeping a wary eye on Haus, the water dog showed him its teeth in a vicious snarl. The thing had caught him by surprise when Haus first came running into the engine room, lurking in the shadows as if waiting to ambush him. Haus figured that hadn't been the water dog's intent. His gut told him that the creature was trying to disable the *Hell-bender* not just find prey. Looking into its glowing, red eyes now Haus could see the intelligence in them. The bloody thing had disarmed him pretty easily in those first moments of their encounter, pinning him against the wall of the engine room, attacking with its mouth and clawed hands while its tail hand snaked down to the holster on his hip, grabbing the pistol there, and flinging it out of his reach. Since then, he'd been fighting the thing hand to hand with only his sheer strength and his boot knife. They had picked at each other enough already. It was time for both of them to end it now, one way or another.

Snarling, the water dog lunged at Haus. He dodged the slashing claws that flashed through the air, catching the creature by the throat with his right hand. Haus slammed the beast into the metal wall of the engine room, muscles bulging on his arm as he held it there. With his left hand, the burly man plunged the blade of his boot knife into the water dog's right eye. The blade ground against the thing's eye socket as he twisted it deeper and deeper, penetrating the monster's brain. The water dog stopped struggling and went limp. Haus released his hold on its throat, letting the monster's body thud onto the floor at his feet.

Brian skidded to a halt as he realized that Tali wasn't following him. He turned to see the medic trying to get Dan up on his feet. Dan was moaning, his chest a mess of slashed up meat. Brian cursed himself for being an idiot. He'd been so caught up in being the hero, charging in with his shotgun booming, that he'd forgotten all about Dan still being alive. Brian hurried back to Tali and Dan, helping her support his weight as they lifted him up between them.

An Ahuizotl leapt over the railing to thud onto the *Hell-bender's* deck behind them. Another of the creatures came bounding around the corner of the wheelhouse blocking their forward path. Caught between the two, carrying Dan, they were screwed.

Rachel sprinted up the steps of the wheelhouse. Suddenly, power surged through the boat, its engine coming to life with a mighty roar.

"Get out of my way!" Rachel yelled at Emma who was still clutching the *Hell-bender's* wheel.

Emma let go of the wheel, scrambling to get out of Rachel's path so that she could take over. Rachel wasn't heading for the wheel though. It was the huge searchlight next to it that Rachel needed. Flicking the searchlight on with a cry of triumph, Rachel swung it around, sweeping its bright beam over the deck of the *Hell-bender*. The water dogs had perked up their heads as the beam first came on, piercing the dimness of the boat's emergency lighting. They howled now, crying out in pain, as Rachel washed the beam over them. Several of the water dogs abandoned their attack on the *Hell-bender* and those aboard her, rushing for her sides to hurl themselves into the river.

"Yeeah!" Captain Eli Richards bellowed, "Drive the bastards back!"

Eli's pistols boomed in rapid succession as he fired at the few water dogs too stubborn to make a run for it like the bulk of their brethren. One of his shots split open the forehead of a water dog. Brain matter leaked from the beast's punctured skull as the fire in its red eyes went out. Another of the creatures died as he put a bullet into its ear. The bullet came bursting out from the other side of the water dog's head leaving a gaping exit hole in its wake.

Tali got into the fight. She let go of her hold on Dan, leaving Brian to support the wounded man's full weight. The medic emptied half of her pistol's magazine into the back of a water dog that was in the process of turning to make its retreat.

Soon there was only a single water dog left aboard the *Hell-bender.* It was atop the wheelhouse and behind the area that Rachel was flooding with light. The water dog lowered its head, growling, red burning eyes locked onto her as if wanting vengeance upon Rachel for driving away its brethren.

Marcus loosed a battle cry, charging the monster He tackled the water dog, taking the beast to the deck under him. Its head whipped around, snapping at the big man. Marcus's right fist smashed into the water dog's jaws sending broken teeth and blood flying. The blow stunned the creature. Marcus seized the moment, smashing one fist after another into the water dog's head, until the beast lay still in a puddle of its own blood beneath him.

****

Captain Eli Richards took the wheel over from

Emma. She had gone to check on everyone else in the wake of the attack. He was glad to do it. Steering the *Hell-bender* helped greatly to settle him down and right now he needed that. The whole mess had left him more keyed up than he wanted to admit. There was a bloodlust inside of Eli that sometimes threatened to consume him. He had to be careful not to loose it when his blood got boiling. It was something about himself that Eli hated and had been the reason he'd left his old life and come to the Amazon in the first place. He supposed they all had their own demons to contend with. That was life.

Things could have been a lot worse. It was a miracle they hadn't lost more people in the battle. They had caught a lucky break thanks to Haus getting the power back on and Rachel's quick thinking. It wasn't normal for the water dogs to attack en masse like they had. The Ahuizotl usually only attacked as individuals or sometimes in pairs. Small groups of them were rare. The virtual army that had come out of the jungle after them tonight was something that Eli had never even heard of before. It worried him. What had drawn the water dogs to them in such numbers?

While Eli pondered a question he couldn't answer, Emma was tending to Marcus's wounds. The big man had been fighting the water dogs hand to hand. He was covered in scratches and even had a few bites that stained his clothes red with blood. Tali was the group's medic but she was busy dealing with Dan. His wounds were far worse than the big man's.

Dan had lapsed into unconsciousness. Emma was glad for that. She couldn't imagine the level of pain he had to be in from the looks of the slashes on his chest. If she looked closely enough, Emma could see the white bone of Dan's ribs through the carnage that Tali was disinfecting and attempting to get bandaged up.

Haus had come up from the engine room and after seeing that the battle was over and things were as safe they could be, found a spot and crashed to grab some Zs.

Rachel sat at the firing controls of the forward fifty caliber, watching the shore, taking the occasional slug from the bottle of Tequila clutched in her left hand. Murphy nervously paced the deck near her. Brian and Olivia were on watch at the stern.

"Could you stop doing that please?" Rachel snapped at Murphy.

He stopped pacing back and forth, standing beside her. "Sorry. I'm just. . ."

"Yeah, I get it," Rachel told him, nodding and taking another swig from her bottle. "You know right before the giant snake got him, Froggy showed me a picture of things like the ones that just attacked us on his phone. The idiot was all excited by it. Thought it would be cool to see one that was real, I think. I didn't believe any of the crap he was trying to tell me. Guess he was right about them being real after all."

"I am still trying to process all this," Murphy said though Rachel wasn't sure if he was really talking to her or himself. "Things like those creatures shouldn't be real. The giant snake. . .that you could make an argument for but those things. . .They weren't natural."

Rachel grunted and shrugged. What the hell did it matter if they were natural or not?

"Murphy, give it a rest," she told him. "Just keep your eyes sharp."

Chris came walking up to them. He looked like crap. Hell, they all did. He was carrying a bag. His hand disappeared into it and reemerged holding a PowerBar. Chris offered it to her.

Rachel shook her head.

"You sure? You need to eat something," Chris said.

Jostling her bottle of Tequila at him, Rachel grinned, "This is all I need right now."

"Copy that," Chris sighed, letting the matter drop.

"I'll happily take that off your hands," Murphy reached for the PowerBar.

Chris handed it to him, watching as Murphy tore into it ravenously.

"This gig has already set a new record," Chris commented.

"Huh?" Murphy managed to get out despite the mouthful he was chewing on.

"Four dead so far and we're not even to the objective yet," Chris explained.

"Got wounded too," Rachel chimed in. "Don't forget that."

"Why the hell did Marcus sign us up for this one anyway?" Chris frowned.

"Why don't you ask him?" Rachel chuckled as a shadow fell over Chris.

"You got a problem with me, Chris?" Marcus's deep voice rumbled.

"No sir!" Chris yelped, snapping to attention.

"Good," Marcus nodded. "Why don't you head over and see if our employer needs some chow?"

"Yes sir!" Chris barked and hurried away.

"You scared the crap out of him," Rachel snorted, laughing so hard she had to brace herself against the fifty caliber to keep from toppling over.

Marcus reached out, snatching the bottle of Tequila from her grasp.

"Hey!" Rachel protested. "That's mine."

"I think you've had enough," Marcus boomed. "If those things come back. . ."

"They aren't coming back," Rachel huffed. "Not tonight anyway. We kicked their butts too bad."

"Uhnnnn," Marcus stumbled, looking as if he might fall over.

Rachel leapt up, steadying him, though she didn't let go of her Tequila. His skin was slicked with sweat and hot to the touch.

"What the hell, sir?" Her eyes went wide. "You're burning up."

"I'm. . . I'm fine," Marcus mumbled, trying to push her away and failing.

"Tali!" Rachel shouted.

The medic heard her and came running. One look at Marcus and Tali seemed to know exactly what was going on.

"He's sick," Tali said.

"No crap," Rachel shot back at her.

"Ladies. . ." Marcus started.

"Shut up!" Both of them snaped at him.

"Dan's been like this since I started treating him," Tali told Rachel. "I just found out Haus has the same symptoms as well."

"Frag," Rachel shook her head. She didn't need Tali's training to make the connection of what was happening to the three men. "Those things. . ."

Tali nodded. "Their claws must have had some sort of toxin on or in them."

"Can you counter it?" Rachel asked.

"I've got some anti-venom in my kit," Tali answered. "Whether or not it will work is anybody's guess."

"Well, trying it is better than standing here doing nothing," Rachel snapped.

"It's risky," Tali shot back at her. "What if. . ."

"Just do it!" Rachel barked. "That's an order!"

"You're drunk," Tali hesitated.

"I'm still second in command here and in case you haven't noticed, Marcus is out of it," Rachel was getting angrier by the second.

It was true. Marcus was so messed up by whatever the wounds he'd gotten from the creatures had put into his system. The big man's weight was getting heavier on Rachel and he was no longer protesting anything they were saying. A low moan escaped him as Rachel glanced up to see that his eyes were partially closed.

"Come on," Rachel told Tali. "Help me get him lowered onto the deck."

Between the two of them, they were able to lay Marcus down gently. As soon as he was down, Tali sprinted away to get her medkit.

"Tali!" Emma shouted, intercepting the medic. "Dan is having some kind of seizure! Haus too!"

"Damn it!" The medic snatched up her kit, slinging it open. She couldn't treat all three of the men at the same time.

As if reading her mind, Rachel yelled, "Marcus first!"

Tali leapt into action. She ran back to the big man, stabbing the needle in her hand into him.

"Whoa!" Rachel challenged her. "I thought. . ."

"It's a new type, military grade," Tali blurted out already shoving herself up to get moving towards Dan. He was the worst and should have been the first to get the shot. Only Dan had stopped moving. His body lay still and blood dribbled from his swollen lips. Emma was kneeling over him and gave Tali a sad shake of her head.

"Haus!" Tali wailed, changing her course. She skidded to a stop next to the burly veteran like a runner sliding into home base. His seizure was a bad one. Haus's entire body arced upwards, spine bending. Chad had rushed over and was trying to hold him down but Haus was just too strong. Tali took her shot, grabbing Haus and ramming the tip of the antivenom needle into him. Haus sucked in a huge gasp of air and went still. His eyes were rolled up to show only white. Tali thumped a fist down on his sternum and leaned over to see if she could feel him breathing on her cheek as her fingers probed his neck searching for a pulse.

Rising up from Haus, Tali was grinning like an idiot. "He's alive!"

"Thank God for that," Rachel grunted and then raised her bottle of Tequila to take another huge swig from it.

****

Marcus's eyes fluttered open. He jerked upright, throwing back the sheet that was over him. A quick glance around the room he was in told the big man exactly where he was. Someone had carried him into the room he'd been using as his quarters aboard the *Hell-bender*. That meant it was all real and not some kind of nightmarish fever dream as the memories of his men being killed rushed through his head.

"Oh good!" Emma's voice called to him from outside of the room. "You're up!"

He watched her enter and saw the tray she carried in her hands.

"Brought you something," she smiled. "Tali says you have to be careful to stay hydrated."

"What a night," Marcus grumbled.

"At least it's over," Rachel said.

Marcus saw the dim sunlight spilling through the porthole window of his quarters. "How long was I out?"

"A few hours," Rachel told him. "You've got

some scratches and other minor stuff but Tali says you'll be good to go as soon as you feel up to it. The poison from those things is the only reason you're in bed at all. That stuff is nasty."

"Haus and Dan got up close and personal with those bastards too. How are they doing?" Marcus asked.

"Haus is fine," Rachel started with the good news before adding, "Dan didn't make it though. He died not long after you went south on us."

Marcus clenched his fists, grinding his teeth in frustration and anger. "Frag it. How many people do we have to lose before this nightmare is over with?"

"Almost half of us already," Rachel painfully reminded him.

She smelt of Tequila and sweat. Her eyes were red and bloodshot. Nothing that happened was her fault. Rachel had to know that. Everything was solely on him. It was his job to bring everyone back alive not hers.

"How's everyone holding up?" Marcus frowned, changing the subject.

"As you'd expect for the most part," Rachel sighed. "Murphy and Chris are bundles of raw nerves just waiting for whatever comes at us next. Tali is running around, all fake smiles and giddiness, trying to make folks feel better. Haus is sleeping, trying to get through the after effects of those things' venom just like you are, and Olivia is keeping to herself. Weirdly, good old Brian is taking all this in his stride. I swear I think he's actually excited to be killing monsters."

Marcus grinned. "Kid wants to be a hero."

"According to Tali, he already is," Rachel smiled back at him. "Says he saved her life last night."

"Good kid," Marcus chuckled. "I knew there was a reason I hired him."

"If you say so," Rachel shrugged.

"What our employer and the captain?" Marcus asked.

"Dr. Wallace is eager to reach our destination. She's been pressing the good captain to get us there faster," Rachel answered. "He has been his seemingly usual self though perhaps a bit more subdued."

"So what kind of E.T.A. are we looking at?" Marcus propped himself up on the bed, feeling a bit better and more steady.

"Captain Richards says he should have us to the drop off point just before nightfall," Rachel frowned.

"Nightfall?" Marcus exhaled loudly, "That figures."

"I felt that same when he told me," Rachel

agreed. "Not gonna be an easy choice to make given the luck we've had on this river so far. Do we spend the night on the *Hell-bender* or just head on out into the jungle? I can guarantee you what Dr. Wallace is gonna want to do."

"It is a tough call," Marcus said, "But it's mine to make not hers."

"Really?" Rachel blinked. "She's the one signing your paycheck too, boss."

Marcus grunted defiantly but didn't argue the point.

"Well, I'll leave you to get some more rest," Rachel told him. "I am sure Tali will be bringing you some food to help get your strength back soon. See you in a few hours, boss."

Marcus watched Rachel leave. He rose up from the bed and walked around the room testing his steadiness on his feet and how he felt overall before sitting down again. The anti-venom had done its job. Marcus felt almost one hundred percent, a few more hours of rest and some food, and he should be there.

****

"I believe we've arrived," Captain Eli Richards said, smirking at Dr. Emma Wallace, Marcus, and Haus who stood with him atop the wheelhouse.

Emma checked the small instrument in her hand and nodded. "Indeed, we have."

The sun was sinking in the sky. Within another hour, maybe an hour and a half, it would be dark.

"Marcus, tell your people to gather up their gear," Emma ordered. "We need to get moving while we still have some light."

"Some light?" Marcus huffed. "Ma'am, it'll be dark before we make it more than a couple of miles at best. Are you sure this is a good idea?"

"What do you mean?" Emma asked.

"The last two nights we've been attacked by whacked out creatures that just frankly have no right to even exist in the real world. Both times, we've lost people and could have lost a lot more. I'm just not sure that leaving this boat and hoofing it through the jungle in the dark is a good idea."

"I see your point and understand what you're saying, Marcus," Emma frowned, "but I'd really like to get moving as fast as we can."

"Spending one more night on this boat isn't going to cost us anything and could save some lives, Doctor," Marcus argued.

"Are you telling me that your crew can't handle it out there?" Emma challenged him.

"I didn't say that," Marcus answered through gritted teeth.

"Good," Emma flashed him a smile. "Go get your people ready and tell your man, Chris, I am going to need him to help me with mine."

"Yes ma'am," Marcus nodded, knowing he had lost the battle. There would be no stopping Emma from having her way without truly putting his foot down and possibly landing himself in breach of contract. He wasn't ready for that yet. She was the one writing the paychecks just like Rachel had said. The boat might be a little safer than being out there in the jungle but staying on it certainly didn't guarantee anything. Hell, for all he knew, the jungle could actually be a lot safer than the river based on how things had gone so far.

Marcus gestured at the captain. "And what about him?"

Eli smiled. "Don't you worry. The *Hell-bender* will be right here when you get back. She's not going anywhere."

He didn't really trust Eli but Marcus kept that to himself. There was no point in bringing it up now. Emma certainly appeared to trust the river boat captain so challenging Eli would only rile her up more than she already was with her goal so close at hand.

Marcus motioned for Haus to follow him as the two of them left Dr. Wallace and the captain at the wheel. They went to round up the others and prepare for their trip in the jungle.

Rachel, Chris, Murphy, Brian, Olivia, and Tali assembled on the deck on the *Hell-bender*. Haus stood facing them, carrying his heavy mini-gun, its even heavier ammo pack strapped to his back. Marcus stood next to the burly man, looking over what was left of his crew. It was hard for Marcus as he thought about all those they had lost already.

"Okay, boys and girls," Haus barked. "You got as much of a clue as to where we're headed as the big man and I do. All we know for sure is that we'll be hoofing it through the jungle and God only knows what will be out there waiting for us. You can bet it won't be anything pretty."

"I want all of you to stay sharp and cool out there," Marcus added. "We need to be prepared for anything, people. You've seen the crap we've come across on this river already. It just makes sense to think the same sort of whacked out, unnatural crap will be in that jungle too."

"Yes sir," the gathered troops chorused.

"Now if there's anything else you need to do before we disembark, I suggest you get it done. We'll be getting off this boat in five," Marcus concluded. "Be ready."

As the others headed off to finish anything they had left to do, Haus turned to Marcus. "That was it? I was expecting some kind of speech or something."

"What more was there to say, Haus?" Marcus shrugged.

"Damned if I know but as pep talks go that one sucked," Haus complained.

Five minutes later, Eli had brought the *Hellbender* as close into the shore as he could. Everyone else loaded up into two small row boats, heading for the shore. If Eli was worried about being left alone, he showed no sign of it. Marcus could see him leaning onto the deck side railing, watching them depart.

****

The boats were left on the river bank, tied there securely, as the group trudged into the jungle. Rachel took point with Haus bringing up the rear. Marcus kept close to Emma. It was their job to keep her safe after all and staying by her side was the best means of ensuring that. The others were spread out in a loose, jagged line as they all marched slowly in the direction Emma had directed them.

"I understand you're tracking the energy from the jewel you're after, Doctor," Marcus said, "But do you have any idea of what we'll be heading into out here?"

"What do you mean?" Emma looked confused.

"Are we expecting to march into a lost city or do you think this jewel of yours will be on top of some sort of Aztec pyramid?" Marcus pressed her. "I am just trying to get a feel for what's coming."

"The honest answer to that question is that I have no idea," Emma admitted. "Not really anyway. There are lots of myths and stories about the jewel. It's hard to say which if any of them are true."

"Best guess?" Marcus asked.

"I think we will find the ruins of a city," Emma answered. "But whether the jewel will be sitting out in the open on an altar or be buried inside a tomb. . . well, that's harder to say."

"I see," Marcus nodded. "And that device you keep fiddling with there, just how accurate do you believe it to be?"

Emma glanced down at the scanner she was carrying and then back at the big soldier. "Are you implying that my gear isn't working?"

"I didn't say that," Marcus kept his voice calm and professional. "I'm merely asking if that thing could be wrong."

"It's doubtful," Emma shook her head. "Without getting deep into the science, let's just say it's made to hone on energy signatures and is currently calibrated to the type the jewel is supposed to emit."

"That begs the question of what exactly is this jewel we're after?" Marcus sighed. Emma had briefed him on the jewel when she hired him. He hadn't truly believed much of what Emma said about it then but after seeing the snake and the water dogs, Marcus was much more open to the seemingly impossible now.

With a sideways look in his direction, Emma frowned. "The jewel is a lot of things to a lot of people - a weapon, a tool, an energy battery, a reality altering, magical talisman, even a source of immortality."

"But what do you believe it is?" Marcus took a moment to wipe at the sweat on his brow. The sun might be close to fully setting but the air remained hot and humid even as the shadows among the trees grew longer and deeper.

"Dr. McKay thought it was partly all of those things," Emma answered.

"That's not what I asked," Marcus said firmly.

"I personally believe that the jewel, whatever it may be, is something too powerful to remain lost out here. It needs to be found and studied. Finding the jewel and bringing it back could possibly truly change the world as we know it, Marcus," Emma told him.

Up ahead of them, Rachel came to an abrupt stop. She motioned for everyone else to do the same and keep their mouths shut.

"Stay here," Marcus whispered to Emma and then crept towards where Rachel stood at the lead of the group's loose column formation.

"What ya got?" Marcus asked Rachel as he came alongside her.

"A fragging bad feeling," Rachel said.

Marcus shot her a stern glance. "That's it?"

Rachel shook her head. "Can't you smell it? There's something dead not far from here."

Sniffing the air, Marcus smelt it too as he caught a whiff of rotting meat.

The big man sighed. "Nothing for it. We can't stop here. At least whatever it is surely has to be dead to smell like that."

"Copy that," Rachel reluctantly agreed and got moving again. The rest of the group followed slowly after her.

The group pressed on through the brush until it opened into a large clearing. There was still just enough sunlight to fully take in the horror of what they had stumbled upon. Scattered all about the clearing were the torn apart and mangled bodies of nearly a dozen tribal natives.

"Holy hell," Rachel muttered before she could stop herself.

"Everyone spread out!" Marcus barked. "Secure this clearing, now!"

His crew did as they were instructed, weapons pointed at the trees surrounding the clearing; they took up firing positions so that anything entering it was in at least one of their kill zones.

Marcus had thought that Dr. Wallace would recoil from the gore of what they had found but she didn't. She hurried to one of the bodies, kneeling down to examine it just as Tali was doing on the other side of the clearing from her. Marcus looked around more closely, noticing that all the bodies were male. Most of them, if not all, appeared to have been carrying weapons when they were attacked. Broken spears and bows lay near the corpses. Her eye caught sight of something, half buried in the grass, that reflected the dying rays of the sun. Whatever it was, the thing was made of metal. Marcus walked closer to the object realizing it was an AK-47. He bent over and picked up the weapon. Where in the hell had a group of natives gotten a Russian assault rifle? Marcus ejected its magazine, examining it to confirm what he already suspected. The weapon had been fired.

"These people died quickly," Tali told him, walking over to where he was stood with the AK-47. "Whatever hit them did it hard and fast."

"They put up a fight though," Haus grunted. "You can see that by just glancing around here."

"It didn't seem to make much difference," Dr. Wallace frowned. "The body I examined. . .its wounds were caused by claws and teeth, not human weapons so if you were thinking another tribe hit them, you can rule that out."

"Same with the one I looked at," Tali confirmed. "These guys were attacked by something that wasn't human."

Both Tali and Dr. Wallace appeared troubled by what they had found to the point that he wondered if there was more that they weren't telling him. He didn't press them on it though.

"You think the water dogs did this?" Marcus asked.

Dr. Wallace shook her head. "Not a chance. They are known for taking the eyes, fingernails, and teeth of their victims not tearing them completely apart like this. And these poor bastards appear to be partly eaten too."

"I have to agree with Emma," Tali nodded.

Haus spoke up out of the blue, "Why aren't there any tracks?"

"What?" Marcus turned towards the burly man.

"While they were checking out the bodies, I looked around too. There are literally no tracks here except for those of these dead guys," Haus told him.

"You think whatever hit them took the time to cover them?" Marcus asked, confused.

"That's not what I am saying," Haus protested. "I am saying whatever hit them just never left any."

"That's crazy," Murphy commented.

"More like impossible," Rachel chimed in. "In a fight like what had to have gone down here, you'd think there would be something more than the damage done to those bodies to tell us what hit them."

Marcus looked over at Dr. Wallace, hoping for an answer.

"I have no explanation for that," she sighed. "But this is a good reminder that we're not out here alone. There's something in this jungle that's hungry and dangerous."

"Ha," Rachel chuckled darkly, "I'd say that describes just about everything in this jungle."

"And what about this?" Marcus held up the AK-47. "Seems pretty crazy for native folks like these to be carrying one around?"

"I'd say that's obvious," Rachel smirked. "When the doc's friend passed through these parts with his crew, something got them, and these guys just picked up afterwards."

"Or maybe they attacked the guy's group," Marcus sighed. "I don't suppose it matters. Somehow it wound up in their hands and they're still dead now. The weapon didn't keep them from being slaughtered."

"That's a wonderful thought," Rachel commented.

"It'll be dark soon," Haus warned. "We can't just stand around here waiting on whatever did this to come back."

"He makes a good point," Rachel had a wry grin on her face. "We'd best get moving again."

Marcus raised a hand in the air gesturing for everyone to get back into formation. "Okay people, let's get it in gear."

The group got started heading south after Dr. Wallace doubled checked the direction the energy readings her device continued to pick up were coming from.

Less than an hour later, after the sun had completely dropped from the sky, a heavy rain rolled in. The ground beneath their feet became mud in a matter of minutes making it too dangerous to continue to press on in the dark. Marcus ordered camp to be made. With the rain, there was no hope of getting a fire started. Tarp shelters were set up to at least spare them from the increasing downpour. The rain was cold and falling straight down. There was no wind. Other than the rain and their movements the jungle was eerily still around them. Marcus found himself praying that they wouldn't be attacked during the night because out in the open as they were, with no fire or real source of light, anything that came for them was going to have some serious advantages against them.

A chill ran along his spine as a cry sounded in the darkness not far from the makeshift shelters they'd set up. Again, Marcus wished for a fire. The cry had been distant but it worried him nonetheless.

Thankfully, whatever was out there kept its distance and the night was uneventful. No one really got much rest and not just from the rotating watch Marcus set up. There was a powerful sense of dread that had crept into all of them, even Dr. Wallace.

The rain finally stopped as the night came to an end and the sun rose above the jungle. The ground remained a muddy mess but nonetheless, they had to get moving again. They'd stayed too long where they were for Marcus's liking. If whatever had killed the natives was still in the area, odds were it already had their scent and if it went hunting for more prey, they'd likely be the logical choice for its next meal.

The day was even muggier than usual. The heat was nigh unbearable. Marcus wiped at the sweat that drenched his hair to keep it from running into his eyes. The others were in no better shape. The entire group was suffering. Dr. Wallace slapped at the bugs that flew around her in the air. There seemed to be no end to the types of insects that wanted to feast upon a person in this cursed jungle.

Just before noon, the wailing cries started up among the trees. It wasn't just one creature crying out but rather a chorus of distinct, inhuman voices. The cries were different to those of the water dogs they had encountered on the river. These were deeper, more guttural. Marcus didn't have a clue what kind of creature could be making them.

Marcus was walking next to Dr. Wallace in the center of the group's loose formation. Strangely, she appeared to be almost excited by the strange cries instead of being spooked by them like everyone else.

"Anything you want to tell me, Doc?" Marcus asked her.

Emma smiled. "We're getting close, real close, to where we're headed."

"And you know that how?" The big man frowned, sure he didn't really want to hear her answer.

"The Chupacabra," Emma told him. "Those are their cries. In some legends they guard jewels and given what we're hearing, I'd say some legends are true."

"Do I even want to you tell me how you know what a Chupacabra sounds like?" Marcus challenged the doctor.

"Honestly, I don't," Emma shrugged. "But

listen to those cries. They're canine in nature but not quite. There's nothing known to live in this region that could make noises like those but a Chupacabra."

"I would tell you that you're crazy, that goat suckers aren't real, but. . ." Marcus took a deep breath.

"But you've seen too much already to discount what I am saying out of hand," Emma finished for the big man. "And you'd be right. I don't think they'll attack us though."

"Oh, and why is that?" Marcus stared at her in disbelief.

"Because we should be reaching the area where the jewel is located before nightfall," Emma said glancing down at the screen of the device she continued taking readings with.

"And the jewel is going to protect us?" Marcus tried to keep the skepticism out of his voice but failed.

"I believe that the energy the jewel emits will keep the Chupacabra away," Emma explained, "Just as ultrasonic noise can be used to drive away mice."

"That's a big gamble to take," Marcus pointed out.

"It's not a gamble at all, Marcus," Emma laughed. "If I am wrong, you and your crew are armed to the teeth professionals. Dealing with a pack of Chupacabras shouldn't be beyond your skill set."

Her answer ticked Marcus off but he couldn't argue it. As the group stopped for lunch, Marcus pulled Haus and Rachel aside to let them in on what Dr. Wallace had shared with him.

"So. . . those things that are following us out there are basically messed up dogs that drink blood?" Haus grunted.

"That's one way to put it," Rachel smirked.

"Look, I don't want to believe her either," Marcus said, "But the fact is it's best to assume she's right, at least until we have proof otherwise."

"And Chupacabra are mortal creatures," Rachel's smirk became a full out grin as she worked the pump of the shotgun in her hands. "That means we can blow the little bastards to hell just like we have everything else so far."

****

The Chupacabra, or whatever was on their trail, followed them throughout the day, sometimes seeming to get much closer and only to fall back. Despite the heat, Marcus was pushing everyone on at the fastest pace he figured they could handle. Dr. Wallace's excitement was obvious as the jungle ahead of them opened into a gigantic, circular clearing. In its center sat a pyramid that stretched upwards towards the sky standing several stories tall. There was nothing else within the clearing though. Even the ground was bare. As the group stood on the edge of the clearing, Marcus took a step into it and knelt down to pick up a handful of the ash-like soil within it. He allowed the fistful of dirt to slide through his fingers.

"What are you thinking?" Rachel asked.

"That this place is dead," Marcus answered. "Dr. Wallace, this energy that the jewel is putting out. . . "

"It's not dangerous," Emma told him. "If you're wondering if it's the cause of what you're looking at there, it's not."

"Then what is?" Marcus demanded. "The ground here looks like somebody fragging nuked it. I'm not taking my people into a place where there could be radiation."

"Don't be an idiot," Emma got angry. "I've told you that the jewel's energy is harmless. There's nothing like what you're afraid of here."

"Then what caused this?" Marcus snarled, picking up another handful of dirt and shaking it at her.

"My best guess is that the pH of the soil is off," Emma shot back at him. "That's what this looks like, not radioactivity. Now you listen to me,

Marcus. I'd stake my entire career, my own life, on this place being safe to enter atmospherically. Maybe there are monsters here but there's no lethal radiation or poisons and I am damned well sick of standing here arguing about it. We're here and it's time to go find what we came for."

Marcus stared at the doctor for a long moment before speaking again. "You're lucky I believe you, Emma, or me and mine would be the hell out of here and heading back for the *Hell-bender*."

"Well, I've had enough of standing here," she said and started towards the pyramid, apparently not giving a damn if he and his were following her or not

Gritting his teeth, Marcus motioned for the others to spread out in a defensive formation around Dr. Wallace and cover her approach to the huge structure. Looking down at the gray soil under his boots as he walked across the clearing, Marcus couldn't shake the feeling that there was something more than he could understand wrong with this place. There was a dreadful, ominous feeling that hung in the air around him. Something he couldn't quite put a finger on haunted him to his core. The sooner they found Dr. Wallace's jewel and got the hell out of this cursed clearing, the better it would be for all of them. His grip on his M4 grew so tight his knuckles turned white.

"We got incoming!" Haus suddenly cried out from his position facing back where they had emerged from the jungle. A chorus of inhuman howls and barks rose from among the trees as something came rushing towards the clearing.

"Wait!" Emma yelled, "Hold your fire!"

"What the hell?" Marcus growled, wondering just why the frag the doctor thought she had any say over what his people did in a situation like this one. . .but then he saw what she must have already known.

The things stopped in their tracks as they reached the edge of the clearing, milling about there, as if held at bay by an invisible barrier. The creatures were both terrifying and sickening to look at. They made Marcus think of hairless hyenas. The eyes of the monstrous things glowed red despite the brightness of the sun above. Their fangs were bared in fierce snarls at the ends of their elongated snouts.

"Boss?" Haus asked, his voice quiet but rough.

"Let them be," Dr. Wallace ordered again. "They won't come into the clearing unless we do something to push them."

"Marcus," he heard Rachel call his name.

"You heard the doc!" Marcus barked. "Hold your fire! We're safe in here. Those things won't come any closer."

"Sure," Rachel quipped, "But you have to wonder what it is exactly that's keeping them out, don't you?"

"Stow it," Marcus told her more angrily than he would have liked. He couldn't help his gruffness though, there was just too much anger and frustration boiling within him.

"Come on," Emma said. "Let's get going."

Leading the way, Emma marched towards the giant structure. In the center of its front side was an enormous stairway and at its top was an open doorway. As they reached the bottom of its steps, Marcus turned to his crew.

"Haus, I want you to stay here," Marcus told the burly man. "Olivia, Chris, Brian, hang back with him. If anything comes into this clearing, blow the hell out of it."

"Yes sir," Haus grinned.

"That wasn't needed," Emma said as they started up the steps to the top of the pyramid. "Like I said, those creatures are scared of this place."

"Maybe they have a reason to be," Marcus met Emma's eyes.

"It's just the energy the jewel is emitting that drives them away," Emma explained.

"You can't be sure of that," Rachel cut in.

"No one asked for your opinion," Emma

snapped.

"Bit touchy, eh?" Rachel muttered under her breath so Dr. Wallace couldn't hear but Marcus and Murphy did. The three of them had fallen a few steps behind Emma. And Tali was behind them all, bringing up the rear.

At the top of the stairs was a doorway that wasn't as wide and large as Marcus thought it would be. It was barely wide enough for two people side by side to enter through, not the gaping maw he'd thought seeing the doorway from below. All that could be seen inside of it was darkness.

Emma started to step into it but Marcus's hand shot out to take her by the shoulder.

"Hold on there, Doc," Marcus cautioned her and then nodded at Rachel. "Light it up in there."

"Copy that," Rachel pulled a pair of flares from her gear. Lighting them up, she flung the flares through the doorway. Much to everyone's surprise, the room inside the top of the pyramid was fairly small. In the center of the room was a raised plate of stone that could only be an altar. Beyond it there was another door that looked to lead down into the depths of the pyramid.

"Alright, people. . ." Marcus began but never got to finish as Rachel cut him off.

"Hold on, boss," she interrupted, "Listen! There's something moving in there."

Everyone stood still and quiet as the noises coming from the doorway that led down behind the altar grew louder. Rachel, Murphy, and Marcus aimed their weapons towards it.

The noises became clearer as they continued to draw closer. They were footsteps. Someone or something was coming up into the room from the depths of the pyramid. The flares were still burning brightly, sparks spraying from them, lighting up the room as a man came stumbling up out of the pyramid.

"McKay!?!?" Emma shouted, recognizing him.

The man's head had been tilted downward towards the floor. His body was bloated and swollen. As she called his name, his face rose up. There were things moving on his skin and beneath it. They wriggled and squirmed.

"Oh God . . ." Emma mumbled, retreating a step.

"What the hell is wrong with him?" Rachel asked.

"Is he dead?" Murphy squealed, taking aim at the stumbling man-thing with his rifle. "Are we fragging fighting zombies now?"

"He's not dead," Tali said firmly.

"What are those things?" Marcus demanded of Emma.

"Those. . .those things," Murphy said, "they're

not just on him, they're inside of him too."

"I don't know what they are!" Emma answered Marcus.

The man, McKay, was slowly lurching towards them.

"Stop right there, mister," Marcus warned.

McKay continued forward as if he hadn't heard the big man at all.

"I ain't kidding around, you fragger," Marcus snarled. "One more step and you'll force my hand."

"He isn't stopping, boss," the sharpness of Rachel's voice betrayed the fear she was feeling.

"Em. . .m. . .a," McKay rasped. As he spoke, white worms slithered from his open mouth, scurrying out to join those already clinging to the flesh of his pale cheeks.

"What happened to you?" Dr. Wallace asked, sheer terror in her eyes as she stared at the man who had once been her mentor and more.

"No. . ." McKay croaked and then spoke again in a language that was not English.

Both Murphy and Dr. Wallace appeared to have understood him but neither looked happy about what they had heard.

McKay's throat suddenly swelled up and outward as if someone were inflating a ball inside of it. The skin there split along the middle but no blood came out of the wound. What did come out was more of the worms.

"Frag this," Marcus swore, squeezing the trigger of his M4. The rifle roared on full auto. A stream of rounds tore into McKay, flinging him backwards as they ripped through his chest and blew gaping, gory exit wounds in his back. The wall behind McKay was splattered with both blood and a gray, slimy pus-like substance.

McKay caught himself, retaining his footing by snaring the edge of the stone altar in the center of the room, some of his fingernails popping loose from the force that he clutched it with. His head turned in Marcus's direction. McKay's eyes were nothing more than masses of writhing worms now and blood mixed with the white pus leaked from the holes Marcus had blown in his body.

Rachel jerked up her shotgun, working the weapon's pump. It thundered, bucking in against her shoulder, as she took her shot. Her aim was dead on. McKay's head blew apart in a shower of white and red gore.

Emma rushed forward towards McKay's collapsing corpse.

Tali, who had been watching everything from the group's rear cried out, "No! Don't go near him!"

It was too late though. Dr. Wallace had

dropped to her knees onto the stone floor at McKay's side. What happened next was almost unbearable to watch and Marcus had to force himself not to look away. The white worms all over the floor around McKay swarmed Dr. Wallace, slithering onto and up her body with impossible speed. Some burrowed through her flesh into her body, others bit and chewed at her skin. She rose up, screaming, frantically slapping at the worms, trying to get them off of her. There were too many though.

Emma slumped to her knees as Marcus watched one of the worms entering her right eye through its corner. The thing just slid into her there, vanishing from sight.

"He called them blood worms," Murphy wailed, looking sick, his eyes bugging.

"What?" Marcus spat. "Who did?"

"The McKay guy!" Murphy pointed at the corpse.

"Those aren't blood worms," Rachel barked. "At least not any kind of them that people like us have ever seen before."

"No, they're certainly not," Tali confirmed.

Emma slumped over, collapsing onto the stone floor.

"We've got to help her," Murphy wailed.

"How?" Marcus grunted.

Tali had shrugged off her pack and was slipping medical gloves onto her hands. "We can't just stand here and not try."

Marcus moved between the medic and where Dr. Wallace lay.

"Tali. . ." He warned her. "Do you even know what you're doing?"

"More than you," she reached out to shove the big man out of her way.

Marcus could have held his ground and not let her but decided that it was Tali's call in this case.

She stepped forward, slinging alcohol from a plastic bottle onto the worms that were on Emma. Marcus imagined he could hear the things shrieking as it landed on them. They retreated from Emma's body, squirming away, across the stone floor.

"God help us," Murphy cried out, backpedaling, as some of the worms came his way.

Rachel stood her ground, raising a booted foot and smashing it down, hard, on the worms slithering in her direction.

Marcus wished for a flamethrower. He didn't have anything like that though. All he could do was retreat like Murphy had.

Tali splashed more alcohol around her, keeping the worms at bay, as she knelt to examine Dr. Wallace with her gloved hands.

"Emma's breathing!" Tali called out, searching for the doctor's pulse with her fingers and found it. "Her pulse is strong but erratic!"

"Quick thinking with the alcohol!" Marcus gave her a sharp nod. "How did you know that would work?"

"I didn't!" Tali answered honestly.

The big man's attention returned to the worms on the floor. They were getting closer and closer to his boots.

"We've got to get out of here!" Marcus shouted. "Is she clean enough for you to move safely?"

"I think so," Tali nodded, pouring the last of the alcohol over Dr. Wallace.

He wanted to rush over and help the medic but knew that was a terrible idea. Marcus watched Tali heave Dr. Wallace up enough to get one of the doc's arms up over her shoulders. Dragging the doctor and watching her step, Tali hurried back to where Marcus and the others were. Rachel was still stomping worms. They squashed and splattered beneath her fury.

Murphy was literally whimpering now.

"Come on!" Marcus yelled, motioning for the rest to follow him. He led them out of the top of the pyramid. Moving to the side, he stopped by the doorway as the others ran by him on down the giant stairwell.

Marcus pulled a grenade from his vest, popped its pin, and lobbed it into the room where the worms were slithering about. The explosion seemed to shake the ancient pyramid then the big man was running too.

The others had stopped at the bottom and he skidded to a halt there as well.

Haus, Brian, Olivia, and Chris were waiting for them there. Brian and Chris rushed forward to help with Dr. Wallace.

"No!" Tali screamed at them. "Stay back!"

The two men obeyed her, keeping their distance.

Rachel had helped Tali with Dr. Wallace otherwise the medic would have never made it down the steps carrying Emma's weight. She let go of Emma for now, stepping away from Tali and the doctor, looking down to make sure there were no worms on her body.

"What's going on?" Haus demanded. "What the hell happened up there?"

"Oh frag, oh frag, oh frag. . . those worms. . .," Murphy muttered where he had collapsed to his knees. He was pale and looked scared out of his mind. Marcus couldn't blame him. The crap they'd just seen would have shaken up anyone who wasn't insane.

Walking over to place a hand on Murphy's

shoulder, Marcus gripped him firmly though his eyes met Haus's. "Get it together, man. It's over."

"Is it?" Murphy looked up at him with wet eyes.

Haus was clearly still waiting for an answer to his question.

Marcus waved him off, signaling that they'd have to talk later.

"I need more antiseptics," Tali said.

Marcus didn't question the medic. He shrugged off his pack, digging his out, and handed it to her. Rachel did the same. Murphy was still so shaken up he didn't even seem to have heard the medic.

"Give them space," Marcus ordered the others.

Tali was closely looking Dr. Wallace over to make sure there were no more worms on her body.

"She's clear," the medic said at last.

"Yeah, sure," Rachel grunted, "except for the ones that went inside of her."

"Marcus. . ." Haus started. Brian, Olivia, and Chris all appeared just as concerned and worried as he was.

"Nothing I can do about those here," Tali spoke before anyone else could. "She'll need a hospital with a lot better gear than what I've got to extract the one that went in her eye."

"You're crazy," Murphy spat, staggering up onto his feet. "We can't take her back with us. She's infected with those worms. We don't even know what the hell those things are!"

"It's our job to see her back safely," Marcus growled. "Anyone got an issue with that, they can take it up with me. Got it?"

No one said anything though Haus shook his head in frustration about not being fully in the loop in regards to what was going on.

Beyond the boundary of the clearing, the Chupacabras were baying and barking as if they somehow sensed their prey would soon be venturing back within their ability to strike at. Marcus knew the beasts weren't going to be easy to deal with.

"When we leave this clearing," Marcus told the others, "we'll need to move fast. Tali?"

"I can't carry her alone," the medic frowned.

Marcus glanced at Haus. The burly veteran shook his head no.

"I am not going to order anyone to help Tali as we don't know exactly what we're dealing with yet but we are going to need someone to help carry Dr. Wallace. Anyone willing to volunteer?" Marcus asked.

No one did.

"Fine," Marcus nodded, accepting where things apparently stood in regards to the doctor. "I'll do it. Haus, you have point. Rachel, I want you on the rear. Everyone, be ready for those things.

They'll likely come at us hard and fast."

Marcus handed Tali his rifle. The medic took it with a nod.

Picking up Dr. Wallace in his arms, Marcus shouted, "Let's move, people!"

The rotating barrels of Haus's mini-gun whined as they started to spin as the burly man took aim at the trio of Chupacabra. Roaring, the mini-gun's stream of high-powered rounds ripped the beasts apart. The creatures never stood a chance. Chunks of meat and bone exploded into the air in splashes of bright red. Haus ran straight through the mess of their remains without slowing down. The rest of the group followed after him on his heels.

Brian's M4 spoke as he opened fire at a Chupacabra that bounded towards the group from its right flank. His bullets tore into the beast's head and shoulders. Blood flew as hot lead punched through flesh and bone. Brain matter was leaking from the creature's punctured skull as it collapsed.

A Chupacabra leaped out of the brush at Rachel as she ran by its hiding place. She spun, shotgun thundering. The force of the blast knocked the creature back away from her, opening up its guts. Red-slicked, purple strands of its innards spilled out of the gaping wound she'd blown in its stomach.

Chris cried out in pain as a Chupacabra's sharp tipped proboscis shot out, stabbing into his left thigh. The strike and pain sent Chris reeling, off balance. He thudded onto the ground sending wet mud splashing upwards. The proboscis throbbed as his blood was sucked out through it. His head swam and felt faint from more than just the sickening sight of the proboscis buried in his flesh. He'd lost his hold on his M4 when he had fallen. The rifle lay just out of his reach. Rather than trying to claw his way towards it, Chris jerked his sidearm free from its holster. More through luck than skill, he fired off a quick round that actually found its target. The bullet severed the Chupacabra's proboscis raining a shower of his own blood mixed with the creature's down over him.

The stump of the severed proboscis whipped back into the Chupacabra's mouth as its throat bulged, making a swallowing motion. The beast was whimpering and turning tail to run as Brian finished it with a burst of rounds from his M4 that shredded the flesh of its back.

"Come on, man!" Brian shouted, grabbing Chris and yanking him to his feet. "We gotta move."

And then as suddenly as the attack started, it seemed to end. Marcus heard the Chupacabras' movement through the brush as the beasts scattered, retreating away from the group. Sweat slicked his brow and Dr. Wallace's body was growing heavy in his arms. There was no one else willing to carry her though. If he wanted to get her to the *Hell-bender,* doing so was on him. The big man trudged on through the jungle, with each step he took growing increasingly harder than the one before it.

****

Captain Eli Richards was utterly unprepared for the horror that had been brought aboard the *Hell-bender.* He stood outside the room where Tali and Marcus had deposited Dr. Wallace. Emma lay on the bed, unmoving, her skin pale with sweat slicking her skin.

"What the hell happened to her that has all of you so freaked out?" Eli asked.

"Parasites," Tali answered, standing next to Emma's bed. "She's infected."

"And you brought her onto my ship without telling me that?" Eli challenged the medic.

"I don't think she's infectious. . .at least not if we're careful," Tali answered.

"If we're careful?" Eli balked.

"Settle down," Marcus warned the captain. "You heard Tali. The doctor won't be a danger to anyone if we keep her in here."

"Right. . ." Eli quipped, "And. . ."

Marcus's hand shot out. Eli was fast enough to see it coming and tried to deflect Marcus's hand aside but failed. The big man was too strong. Fingers closing around Eli's neck, Marcus lifted him from the floor and slammed his back against the wall. The impact was almost enough to knock the wind out of his lungs.

"Captain, I'll only say this once," Marcus bellowed, his deep voice rumbling with violence, "Our job is to make sure nothing happens to her and your job is to get us home. Did we screw up? Sure. That doesn't change anything though. Tali thinks Emma can be saved and I am going to make sure she gets a chance for that to happen. Your job hasn't changed either and you're not going to screw up, Captain. You're going to get us back to the village we embarked from. Until then, you'll damn well stay out of my way. Do I make myself clear?"

Marcus released Eli. The captain slid down the wall to the floor. Eli stood there rubbing at his throat. He glared up at the big man but didn't say anything more.

"Good," Marcus grunted. "Glad we got that settled."

Eli left the room without looking back leaving Tali and Marcus alone with Dr. Wallace. Marcus closed the door after him.

"You were a bit rough with him, don't ya think? This is his ship after all," Tali commented. "It's not like you to be so . . .angry."

"Tali," Marcus said stepping closer to the medic. "Tell me the truth, is she really going to be okay?"

"If we get her help in time," Tali shrugged, "Maybe."

Dr. Wallace stirred.

"Emma?" Tali asked, looking down at her on the bed as Marcus made his move. She never saw it coming. There was no time to scream or chance to fight back. The big man grabbed her lower jaw with one hand and her throat with the other. Wrenching her mouth wide, he opened his own. An eruption of white worms, like projectile vomit, sprayed from his mouth into hers.

Tali gagged as the worms squirmed and wiggled, forcing themselves down her throat. Then just like that, it was over. The worms that hadn't gone directly into her mouth and had fallen to the floor of the room slithered away, vanishing into the shadows. Tali pulled free of Marcus, swallowing over and over, her head moving oddly from the motion. The medic staggered sideways, dropping onto the edge of the bed. Emma was fully conscious now and sat up to give Tali room there. The doctor caught the medic as Tali collapsed the rest of the way over, gently lying her flat.

Marcus towered over Emma where she sat on the bed. She raised her head to look at him, white worms moving and twisting about across her eyes and beneath their lids. A series of inhuman clicking noises rang out from her mouth.

"I understand," Marcus nodded. "I'll get it done."

Emma clicked at him again and returned her attention to Tali, reaching out to run her fingers through the medic's hair with an almost loving gentleness.

Marcus wheeled about and marched from the room into the corridor beyond it, pausing only to make sure the door was closed tightly behind him.

****

Eli, shaken up by his encounter with Marcus, had returned to the *Hell-bender's* wheel. He flipped a switch, drawing up the boat's heavy anchors and getting her ready to move. Kicking her engine into gear, Eli steered out away from the shore, making a turn to bring her about.

"You okay?" a gruff voice asked from behind him.

Looking over his shoulder, Eli saw Haus approaching him at the wheel.

Eli turned to face the burly man head on. "You come to give me crap too?"

"What the hell you talking about?" Haus asked, confused.

"Your boss just put me in my place," Eli scowled. "He treats me like that again and. . ."

"Whoa," Haus let go of his hold on the mini-gun he carried, allowing the weapon to sling from its strap, and held up his hands, palms out, in a gesture of surrender. "You need to calm the frag down there, Captain."

With blinding speed, Eli drew the pistol holstered on his right hip, aiming its barrel at the burly man's forehead. "Now you're going to boss me around on my own boat too?"

Haus didn't flinch but the burly man went completely serious, his voice calm and level. "Captain, I think you need to lower that weapon."

"Do you?" Captain Richards sighed.

"Don't suppose it really matters," Haus shrugged. "You're the one with the gun."

Spinning his pistol around on his finger, Eli holstered the weapon.

"I reckon' we've lost enough people already," Eli frowned. "I don't feel like adding to the list."

"Thanks," Haus laughed. He slapped Eli on the back as the captain turned to grip the *Hell-bender's* wheel again.

"Not looking forward to more nights on this river," Haus looked out at the murky water ahead of the boat's bow. "I've seen enough monsters for one lifetime. I mean, bloody hell, before this gig, I wouldn't have believed any of the crap we've run into existed."

"There are more things in Heaven and Earth. . ." Eli said quietly.

"Hey!" Marcus's voice boomed as the big man came walking up to them.

Eli ignored him, keeping his eyes on the boat's course.

"How's the doc doing?" Haus asked.

"Dr. Wallace is recovering," Marcus barked. "I ordered Tali to stay and keep an eye on her."

"We're down a lot of people," Haus shook his head. "And we both know just how deadly this river is now."

"Nightfall is coming. Get everyone together," Marcus growled at Haus. "We need to have a talk about how things are going to work from here on out."

"Yes sir," Haus nodded.

Marcus stomped away, leaving both Haus and Eli watching the big man go.

Eli noticed that Haus appeared somewhat thrown off by what had just happened between himself and Marcus.

"He's not the same man as he was," Eli commented.

Haus did flinch now at those words. He glanced around at the captain, his brow furrowing in thought. "That's a pretty spot on assessment."

"You better get going, Haus," Eli warned the burly veteran. "I think your boss is done putting up with anything that doesn't go his way."

Alone again, Eli thought about what he'd just told Haus. Marcus had truly changed from the man he'd first met. Sure, the big guy had been through hell, thrown up against monsters he'd never dreamt of, but Eli wondered if there was more going on than that. Mentioning what he was thinking to Haus seemed like a very bad idea. The burly veteran was zealously loyal to Marcus. You could see it between them every time they interacted. No. It was best to keep his suspicion to himself for now. If those suspicions proved to be true. . . He'd deal with it then.

What worried him right now was the doctor. Since he had met Emma, Eli admitted to himself that, on some level, he was falling for her. The two of them had chemistry from that first moment their eyes met. Neither of them had really acted on the feelings they seemed to share, both keeping their relationship limited to professionalism touched by a few instants of growing friendship.

Marcus and Tali hadn't exactly been super forthcoming with details about what had happened to her out there during their hunt for the jewel. All he knew for sure was that Emma was infected with some sort of contagious parasite and he was dang sure it wasn't a kind of parasite that had ever been encountered before, at least by Tali. Eli truly cared about Emma but he also cared about making it back alive.

With a sigh, Eli enabled the *Hell-bender's* auto guidance and navigation system and left the wheel. Haus had gathered the others on the main deck. Chris, Brian, Olivia, and Rachel stood with the burly man waiting on Marcus to show up. He and Dr. Wallace emerged from the *Hell-bender's* interior. Eli stopped in his tracks, halfway down the stairs to the deck, frozen by the shock of seeing Emma up and about.

"Doctor," Rachel said, just as confused and stunned by Emma's appearance with Marcus as Eli was. "I'm glad to see you're better."

Haus kept quiet, his eyes on Emma.

"So, boss, you about to give us the old don't get your arse killed speech?" Brian quipped.

"Not exactly," Marcus grinned. "Go ahead, Dr. Wallace. Tell them what you told me."

"The jewel I spent my entire life chasing was nothing more than a fiction, a tale made up to lure those like myself to the great temple of the Dwellers," Dr. Wallace explained.

"The Dwellers?" Chris asked.

"Yes," Dr. Wallace purred, "the Dwellers. For thousands of years, they have slept within their temple, waking only to prey upon those bold or foolish enough to enter it. . . that was until my mentor Dr. McKay arrived. His arrival in the temple changed. . .everything."

"Cute Shatner pauses there, Doc," Brian laughed. "We in an episode of Star Trek now?"

"Brian!" Marcus roared, an almost primal anger flaring in his eyes.

"Yes sir!" Brian barked, snapping to attention and shutting his mouth.

Dr. Wallace cleared her throat and then continued, "The Dwellers no longer wish to remain isolated from the world."

"And what does that matter to us?" Rachel asked as Marcus glared at her.

"That is a good question, Rachel," Dr. Wallace smirked. "The answer is that we are going to set them free."

"What?" Haus blurted out. "Why the hell. . .?"

Before Haus could say anything else, Dr. Wallace opened her mouth, her jaw unhinging like a snake's. From it sprayed a blast of grayish-white fluid filled with worms. Rachel tried to throw herself out of its path but was too slow. A splatter of the worm goo struck her left cheek. Chris, who was also hit by it, was screaming. Worms bit and gnawed into his flesh, entering his body. He slumped to the deck, head tilting back and eyes rolling up to show only whites. . .and slithering worms.

Eli's heart shattered as he saw what Emma had become. She was no longer human, a carrier of a dread pestilence that she hoped to unleash upon the world of man.

Haus didn't have his mini-gun. He yanked his sidearm free of its holster, taking aim at Dr. Wallace. Marcus came plowing into him like a giant linebacker. One of his huge hands caught Haus's gun arm by the wrist, yanking it upwards. The pistol went off firing a shot that ricocheted from the deck's railing with a sharp clang. Haus's back thudded onto the deck, knocking the breath from his lungs, as Marcus's weight came down on top of him. The two men wrestled, Haus trying to get free, as Marcus's mouth slowly opened and unhinged. Haus could see dozens upon dozens of the white worms moving about inside of it, some of them crawling out to slither up along the curves of Marcus's cheeks.

Brian, who had brought his M4 with him, let loose on full auto at Dr. Wallace.

"No!" Eli yelled at the top of his lungs, revealing his presence watching them all on the stairs.

Emma's body shook and jerked as the rounds from Brian's M4 ripped into it. No blood rushed forth from the wounds they made only more of the white pus that she had vomited onto Rachel and Chris. Brian's burst of fire came to an end as his M4 clicked empty. He blinked, dismayed, seeing that Dr. Wallace was still standing. Hissing, worms dangling from her lips and out of her wounds, Dr. Wallace stomped towards Brian. He ejected his M4's spent mag and rammed another one into the weapon just as Dr. Wallace reached him. Snatching the rifle from his hands, she effortlessly snapped it in half, flinging its pieces in opposite directions. Brian reeled backwards, trying to get away from the doctor. Lunging forward, her right hand caught his shoulder. Its fingers dug deep into his flesh. Brian cried out in pain, bringing his knee up into Dr. Wallace's groin as she pulled him closer. The blow knocked the doctor off balance just enough for Brian to wrench free of her grasp. Looking at his shoulder, he saw the red of his blood seeping up through the holes she'd torn in his shirt and the meat below it. . . but that wasn't all he saw. The last wriggling bit of a white worm squirmed into him through the wound.

At first Brian didn't feel the thing but then almost as if the worm had detonated within him like a tiny fragmentation grenade, his entire shoulder and arm were wracked by burning pain. He screamed, stumbling up against the railing of the deck. Dr. Wallace had recovered from the blow he'd dealt her and was coming at him again. Her eyes were gone now, as if eaten away, replaced by orbs of twisting, entwining masses of white. Seeing his own future in those horrific orbs, Brian drew his sidearm and pressing the cold metal of its barrel to the underside of his chin, pulled the pistol's trigger.

The bullet exited through the top of his skull in an explosion of red and white fluids mixed with fragments of bone. His corpse teetered over the railing and then dropped with a loud splash into the river below the boat.

"Hey!" Olivia shouted, leveling the barrel of the pump action shotgun in her hands at Dr. Wallace. "It's your turn now, witch!"

The shotgun boomed, echoing in the gloom of the falling night. A huge hole was blown straight through Dr. Wallace's abdomen. Olivia could see the deck railing through it. Yet still, the infected woman didn't fall.

Haus managed to shove Marcus's head to the side away from him as the big man vomited a stream of white worms. They splattered onto the deck near Haus. Knowing they'd come for him, Haus heaved with all his might, rolling himself and Marcus with him, away from the worms. There was just no breaking the big man's hold on him. Marcus had always been strong but it was as if the things inside of him were boosting his strength to a superhuman level. Haus kept struggling against Marcus as the big man brought his head around. Staring up into a mass of white worms, there was no escape this time. Haus screamed as Marcus puked them onto him.

Rachel had drawn her boot knife. It was drenched in her own blood as was the deck beneath where she slouched against the deck's railing. Her cheek was a mass of mangled flesh as Rachel continued to cut into it with the blade of the knife. Face tight from pain, she reached up to grab the wriggling tails of worms attempting to get deeper inside of her. She wrenched them free, flinging them away. It was a fool's effort and Rachel was quickly coming to realize that. There were too many in her already and too deep to cut out. Accepting her fate, Rachel hauled herself up and leaped towards where Haus was thrashing about with Marcus pinning him to the deck. Flinging herself onto Marcus's back, she grabbed his head by the hair, yanking it farther back, exposing the big man's neck. Her blade slashed across it, loosing even more worms in an explosion of white fluid over Haus. There was nothing she could do about that, he was already infected anyway. Rachel's singular goal was to put Marcus down. She owed him that much and knew it was what he'd want if his mind were still his own.

Despite the large amount of white fluid flowing from his open neck, Marcus rose up, lifting Rachel from the deck with him. His huge hands reached around his back to claw her, trying to tear her loose from him. Rachel slammed the blade of her knife deep into the side of Marcus's skull. *That* did the trick. Marcus toppled over and crashed onto the deck with a loud thud as Rachel jumped off of his falling corpse. He lay there, unmoving, as hundreds of worms slithered out of his body through all of its openings. Rachel stomped at the worms, squishing as many of the things as she could with the soles of her boots until, without warning, Haus's hand caught her left ankle. With a jerk, he pulled her off balance. Rachel hit the deck hard, her head slamming against its wood. Her vision blurring, the last thing Rachel saw was Haus crawling onto her.

Olivia worked the pump of her shotgun, chambering another round, as Dr. Wallace calmly walked towards her, despite the gaping hole in her stomach.

"You cannot stop us," Dr. Wallace hissed with worms squirming over her teeth and lips.

"No but I can!" Eli shouted, jumping from the stairs of the wheelhouse onto the main deck. He gestured for Olivia to make a run for it.

After finally being able to tear his eyes away from the unfolding horror of the battle, he'd raced to his quarters in order to get the flamethrower that he now wore strapped to his back and was ready to join the fight. Eli squeezed the weapon's trigger and held it tight. A geyser of flame erupted, spraying outward to wash over Dr. Wallace. The fire burnt away her flesh as Emma wailed like a banshee, sinking to her knees.

Eli jerked the flamethrower around, taking aim at Haus and Rachel. He hosed them as well then began sweeping the barrel back and forth until the entire main deck of the *Hell-bender* was ablaze. Eli retreated up the stairs of the wheelhouse with Olivia. The smoke was thick as they reached the top of the wheelhouse and looked down into the inferno below them.

"Is it over?" Olivia asked.

"Yeah," Eli nodded, "I think it is."

Without warning, Tali and Murphy came shrieking out of the shadows at them. Olivia spun to meet them, her shotgun thundering at point blank range. The shot she fired reduced Murphy's head to a shower of white pus that splattered over her.

Eli dodged Tali's lunge, sidestepping her charge, and slammed the nozzle of his flamethrower into her back. The blow sent her flying from the top of the wheelhouse into the flames below. He looked around to see Murphy's headless corpse, lying, twitching, at Olivia's feet.

"You okay?" he asked.

"I'm fine," Olivia said, wiping away white pus from the side of her face with the backside of her hand.

Eli wanted to believe her, knowing he couldn't take that chance.

"No! Don't. . ." Olivia yelled as Eli raised the nozzle of his flamethrower at her.

He didn't give her the chance to say anything more. The flamethrower roared as he doused her with flames. Olivia stumbled backwards as the fire burnt away her hair and flesh, the fat of her body popping and sizzling as Eli continued to pour on the flames. Then, it was all over. . .

Eli quickly roasted the worms around Murphy's corpse, setting the dead man's body on fire in the process then shut the flamethrower down. He shrugged its heavy pack from his back and stood atop the wheelhouse looking around at the destruction which surrounded him. Sweat slicked his skin from the heat of the flames that continued to burn and spread over the rest of the *Hell-bender*. Eli thought about running, trying to get off the boat before the fire reached its fuel and the whole thing blew but couldn't bring himself to do it. There was no way he could know for sure that he wasn't infected too with the intelligent worms simply lying dormant inside of him.

"God forgive me. God forgive us all," he said aloud before the *Hell-bender* exploded.

The burning boat drifted upon the current of the river like a Viking funeral pyre with nothing left alive aboard it.

The End

Author Bio

Eric S Brown is the author of numerous book series including the Bigfoot War series, the Psi-Mechs Inc. series, the Kaiju Apocalypse series (with Jason Cordova), the Crypto-Squad series (with Jason Brannon), the Homeworld series (With Tony Faville and Jason Cordova), the Jack Bunny Bam series, and the A Pack of Wolves series. Some of his stand alone books include War of the Worlds plus Blood Guts and Zombies, Casper Alamo (with Jason Brannon), Sasquatch Island, Day of the Sasquatch, Bigfoot, Crashed, World War of the Dead, Last Stand in a Dead Land, Sasquatch Lake, Kaiju Armageddon, Megalodon, Megalodon Apocalypse, Kraken, Alien Battalion, The Last Fleet, and From the Snow They Came to name only a few. His short fiction has been published hundreds of times in the small press in beyond including markets like the Onward Drake and Black Tide Rising anthologies from Baen Books, the Grantville Gazette, the SNAFU Military horror anthology series, and Walmart World magazine. He has done the novelizations for such films as Boggy Creek: The Legend is True (Studio 3 Entertainment) and The Bloody Rage of Bigfoot (Great Lake films). The first book of his Bigfoot War series was adapted into a feature film by Origin Releasing in 2014. Werewolf Massacre at Hell's Gate was the second of his books to be adapted into film in 2015. Major Japanese publisher, Takeshobo, bought the reprint rights to his Kaiju Apocalypse series (with Jason Cordova) and the mass market, Japanese language version was released in late 2017. Ring of Fire Press has released a collected edition of his Monster Society stories (set in the New York Times Best-selling world of Eric Flint's 1632). In addition to his fiction, Eric also writes an award-winning comic book news column entitled "Comics in a Flash" as well a pop culture column for Altered Reality Magazine. Eric lives in North Carolina with his wife and two children where he continues to write tales of the hungry dead, blazing guns, and the things that lurk in the woods.

Check out other great

Cryptid Novels!

J.H. Moncrieff

RETURN TO DYATLOV PASS

In 1959, nine Russian students set off on a skiing expedition in the Ural Mountains. Their mutilated bodies were discovered weeks later. Their bizarre and unexplained deaths are one of the most enduring true mysteries of our time. Nearly sixty years later, podcast host Nat McPherson ventures into the same mountains with her team, determined to finally solve the mystery of the Dyatlov Pass incident. Her plans are thwarted on the first night, when two trackers from her group are brutally slaughtered. The team's guide, a superstitious man from a neighboring village, blames the killings on yetis, but no one believes him. As members of Nat's team die one by one, she must figure out if there's a murderer in their midst—or something even worse—before history repeats itself and her group becomes another casualty of the infamous Dead Mountain.

Gerry Griffiths

CRYPTID ZOO

As a child, rare and unusual animals, especially cryptid creatures, always fascinated Carter Wilde. Now that he's an eccentric billionaire and runs the largest conglomerate of high-tech companies all over the world, he can finally achieve his wildest dream of building the most incredible theme park ever conceived on the planet... CRYPTID ZOO. Even though there have been apparent problems with the project, Wilde still decides to send some of his marketing employees and their families on a forced vacation to assess the theme park in preparation for Opening Day. Nick Wells and his family are some of those chosen and are about to embark on what will become the most terror-filled weekend of their lives—praying they survive. STEP RIGHT UP AND GET YOUR FREE PASS... TO CRYPTID ZOO

Check out other great

Cryptid Novels!

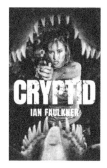

Ian Faulkner

CRYPTID

Be careful what you look for. You might just find it.1996. A group of 14 students walked into the trackless virgin forests of Graham Island, British Columbia for a three-day hike. They were never seen again. 2019. An American TV crew retrace those students' steps to attempt to solve a 23-year-old mystery.A disparate collection of characters arrives on the island. But all is not as it seems. Two of them carry dark secrets. Terrible knowledge that will mean death for some – but a fighting chance of survival for others. In the hidden depths of the forests – man is on the menu. Some mysteries should remain unsolved...

Eric S. Brown

LOCH NESS HORROR

The Order of the Eternal Light, a secret organization have foretold the end of the human race. In order to save all humanity, agents of the Order must locate the Loch Ness Monster and obtain a sample of its blood for within in it is the key to stopping the apocalypse but finding the monster will be no easy task.

Check out other great
Cryptid Novels!

Hunter Shea

THE DOVER DEMON

The Dover Demon is real...and it has returned. In 1977, Sam Brogna and his friends came upon a terrifying, alien creature on a deserted country road. What they witnessed was so bizarre, so chilling, they swore their silence. But their lives were changed forever. Decades later, the town of Dover has been hit by a massive blizzard. Sam's son, Nicky, is drawn to search for the infamous cryptid, only to disappear into the bowels of a secret underground lair. The Dover Demon is far deadlier than anyone could have believed. And there are many of them. Can Sam and his reunited friends rescue Nicky and battle a race of creatures so powerful, so sinister, that history itself has been shaped by their secretive presence? "THE DOVER DEMON is Shea's most delightful and insidiously terrifying monster yet." – Shotgun Logic Reviews "An excellent horror novel and a strong standout in the UFO and cryptid subgenres." –Hellnotes "Non-stop action awaits those brave enough to dive into the small town of Dover, and if you're lucky, you won't see the Demon himself!" – The Scary Reviews PRAISE FOR SWAMP MONSTER MASSACRE "B-horror movie fans rejoice, Hunter Shea is here to bring you the ultimate tale of terror!" – Horror Novel Reviews "A nonstop thrill ride! I couldn't put this book down." – Cedar Hollow Horror Reviews

Armand Rosamilia

THE BEAST

The end of summer, 1986. With only a few days left until the new school year, twins Jeremy and Jack Schaffer are on very different paths. Jeremy is the geek, playing Dungeons & Dragons with friends Kathleen and Randy, while Jack is the jock, getting into trouble with his buddies. And then everything changes when neighbor Mister Higgins is killed by a wild animal in his yard. Was it a bear? There's something big lurking in the woods behind their New Jersey home. Will the police be able to solve the murder before more Middletown residents are ripped apart?

Printed in Great Britain
by Amazon

WINNIE~THE~POOH

GLOOM & DOOM
FOR PESSIMISTS

EGMONT

We bring stories to life

First published in 2018 by Egmont UK Limited
The Yellow Building, 1 Nicholas Road, London W11 4AN
www.egmont.co.uk

Additional text by Catherine Shoolbred
Designed by Pritty Ramjee

ISBN 978 1 4052 9111 8
68619/001
Printed in the UK

WINNIE~THE~POOH

GLOOM & DOOM
FOR PESSIMISTS

A.A.MILNE

with decorations by E.H.SHEPARD

EGMONT

INTRODUCTION

The old grey donkey, Eeyore, stood by himself in a thistly corner of the Forest, his front feet well apart, his head on one side, and thought about things.

Are you like Eeyore, a deep-thinker, whose mind often turns to the gloomy side of things? If you tend to be a little cynical and often view life as a glass half empty, then you may recognise yourself in this collection of pessimistic moments experienced by Eeyore and his friends in the Hundred Acre Wood.

Sometimes you just don't feel like sunshine and happiness …

'And how are you?' said Winnie - the - Pooh.
Eeyore shook his head from side to side.
'Not very how,' he said. 'I don't seem
to have felt at all how for a long time.'
'Dear, dear,' said Pooh, 'I'm sorry about that.'

... AND YOU'RE NOT ALWAYS IN THE MOOD FOR FUN AND GAMES.

'Good morning, Eeyore,' said Pooh.

'Good morning, Pooh Bear,' said Eeyore gloomily.

'If it is a good morning,' he said. 'Which I doubt,' said he.

'Why, what's the matter?'

'Nothing, Pooh Bear, nothing. We can't all, and some
of us don't. That's all there is to it.'

'Can't all what?' said Pooh, rubbing his nose.

'Gaiety. Song‑and‑dance. Here we go round
the mulberry bush.'

AS YOU GET OLDER, YOUNGER PEOPLE SEEM TO GET LOUDER ...

'Hush!' said Eeyore in a terrible voice to all
Rabbit's friends-and-relations, and 'Hush!'
they said hastily to each other all down
the line, until it got to the last one of all.'

... AND THE TIME COMES WHEN YOU LOOK IN THE MIRROR AND DON'T RECOGNISE YOURSELF.

*[Eeyore] looked at himself in the water.
'Pathetic,' he said. 'That's what it is. Pathetic.'
He turned and walked slowly down the stream
for twenty yards, splashed across it, and walked
slowly back on the other side. Then he looked at
himself in the water again. 'As I thought,' he said.
'No better from this side.'*

KEEP YOUR EXPECTATIONS LOW AND YOU'LL NEVER BE DISAPPOINTED.

'Eeyore,' said Owl, 'Christopher Robin is giving a party.'
'Very interesting,' said Eeyore. 'I suppose they will be
sending me down the odd bits which got trodden on.
Kind and Thoughtful. Not at all, don't mention it.'

———◆———

No one likes being the last to know.

And two days later Rabbit happened
to meet Eeyore in the Forest.
'Hallo, Eeyore,' he said, 'what are you looking for?'
'Small, of course,' said Eeyore. 'Haven't you any brain?'
'Oh, but didn't I tell you?' said Rabbit. 'Small
was found two days ago.'
There was a moment's silence.
'Ha-ha,' said Eeyore bitterly. 'Merriment and
what-not. Don't apologize. It's just what would happen.'

PLAIN SPEAKING IS UNDERRATED.

'I've got a sort of idea,' said Pooh at last,
'but I don't suppose it's a very good one.'
'I don't suppose it is either,' said Eeyore.
'Go on, Pooh,' said Rabbit. 'Let's have it.'
'Well, if we all threw stones and things into
the river on one side of Eeyore, the stones
would make waves, and the waves would
wash him to the other side.'
'That's a very good idea,' said Rabbit,
and Pooh looked happy again.
'Very,' said Eeyore. 'When I want to be
washed, Pooh, I'll let you know.'

WE CAN'T ALL LIVE IN A SOCIAL WHIRL ...

'Here it is!' cried Christopher Robin excitedly.
'Pass it down to silly old Pooh. It's for Pooh.'
'For Pooh?' said Eeyore.
'Of course it is. The best bear in all the world.'
'I might have known,' said Eeyore. 'After all,
one can't complain. I have my friends. Somebody
spoke to me only yesterday. And was it last week
or the week before that Rabbit bumped into me
and said, "Bother!" The Social Round.
Always something going on.'

... AND WHY SOCIALISE WHEN PEOPLE ARE SO INCONSIDERATE?

Eeyore ... looked round at them in his melancholy way. 'I suppose none of you are sitting on a thistle by any chance?'
'I believe I am,' said Pooh. 'Ow!' He got up, and looked behind him. 'Yes, I was. I thought so.'
'Thank you, Pooh. If you've quite finished with it ... It doesn't do them any Good, you know, sitting on them,' he went on, as he looked up munching. 'Takes all the Life out of them. Remember that another time, all of you. A little Consideration, a little Thought for Others, makes all the difference.'

SOMETIMES IT FEELS LIKE PEOPLE DON'T UNDERSTAND YOU ...

Piglet explained to Tigger that he mustn't mind
what Eeyore said because he was always gloomy;
and Eeyore explained to Piglet that, on the contrary,
he was feeling particularly cheerful this morning.

...≈...

... OR WANT YOU AROUND.

'That's right, Eeyore. Drop in on any of
us at any time, when you feel like it.'
'Thank-you, Rabbit. And if anybody says
in a Loud Voice, "Bother, it's Eeyore,"
I can drop out again.'
Rabbit stood on one leg for a moment.
'Well,' he said, 'I must be going. I am
rather busy this morning.'

Sometimes you prefer
to be left alone ...

'That's what I call bouncing,' said Eeyore.
'Taking people by surprise. Very unpleasant
habit. I don't mind Tigger being in the Forest,'
he went on, 'because it's a large Forest, and
there's plenty of room to bounce in it. But
I don't see why he should come into my
little corner of it, and bounce there.'

... ALTHOUGH
SAYING GOODBYE
CAN BE HARD.

'Hallo, everybody,' said Christopher Robin
– 'Hallo, Pooh.'
They all said 'Hallo,' and felt awkward and
unhappy suddenly, because it was a sort of
good-bye they were saying, and they didn't
want to think about it. So they stood around,
and waited for somebody else to speak, and
they nudged each other, and said, 'Go on.'

IT'S LITTLE WONDER THAT LIFE BRINGS OUT THE PESSIMIST IN YOU.

'Good morning, Eeyore,' shouted Piglet.
'Good morning, Little Piglet,' said Eeyore. 'If it is
a good morning,' he said. 'Which I doubt,' said he.
'Not that it matters,' he said.

YOU MAY FIND SARCASM COMES MORE NATURALLY TO YOU THAN TO OTHERS ...

'I didn't know you were playing,' said Roo.

'I'm not,' said Eeyore.

'Eeyore, what are you doing there?' said Rabbit.

'I'll give you three guesses, Rabbit.

Digging holes in the ground? Wrong. Leaping
from branch to branch of a young oak-tree? Wrong.
Waiting for somebody to help me out of the river?
Right. Give Rabbit time, and he'll always
get the answer.'

... AND YOU PREFER TO AVOID THE OVERLY~OPTIMISTIC TYPE.

'That's right,' said Eeyore.
'Sing. Umty~tiddly, umpty~too.
Here we go gathering Nuts
and May. Enjoy yourself.'
'I am,' said Pooh.
'Some can,' said Eeyore.

THERE ARE OFTEN RAIN CLOUDS ON THE HORIZON ...

'Hallo, Eeyore!' said Roo.
Eeyore nodded gloomily at him. 'It will
rain soon, you see if it doesn't,' he said.
Roo looked to see if it didn't and it didn't.

... OR WORSE.

'It's snowing still,' said Eeyore gloomily.

'So it is.'

'And *freezing*.'

'Is it?'

'Yes,' said Eeyore. 'However,' he said,
brightening up a little, 'we haven't
had an earthquake lately.'

YOU SHOULD AVOID BEING A VICTIM OF ANTISOCIAL BEHAVIOUR.

'How did you fall in, Eeyore?' asked Rabbit,
as he dried him with Piglet's handkerchief ...
'I was BOUNCED,' said Eeyore.
'Oo,' said Roo excitedly, did somebody push you?'
'Somebody BOUNCED me. I was just thinking
by the side of the river – thinking, if any of you
know what that means – when I received
a loud BOUNCE.'

It seems as though you
can't leave something for
a minute without somebody
making off with it.

'The really exciting part,' said Eeyore in his most
melancholy voice, 'is that when I left it this
morning it was there, and when I came back
it wasn't. Not at all, very natural, and it was
only Eeyore's house. But still I just wondered.'

x

Do you ever feel like you're stuck in a rut?

'A week!' said Pooh gloomily. 'What about meals?'

'I'm afraid no meals,' said Christopher Robin,

'because of getting thin quicker. But we will read to you.'

Bear began to sigh, and then found he couldn't

because he was so tightly stuck; and a tear rolled

down his eye, as he said: 'Then would you read

a Sustaining Book, such as would help and comfort

a Wedged Bear in Great Tightness?'

So for a week Christopher Robin read that sort

of book at the North end of Pooh, and Rabbit

hung his washing on the South end.

IF YOU'RE HAVING A BAD DAY, YOU MAY BE BETTER OFF RETREATING TO YOUR BED ...

Then Piglet saw what a Foolish Piglet he had been, and he was so ashamed of himself that he ran straight off home and went to bed with a headache.

... BUT EVEN THOUGH YOU MAY
FEEL BAD ABOUT YOURSELF,
OTHERS SEE THE GOOD IN YOU.

'I see now,' said Winnie-the-Pooh.
'I have been Foolish and Deluded,' said he,
'and I am a Bear of No Brain at All.'
'You're the Best Bear in All the World,'
said Christopher Robin soothingly.
'Am I?' said Pooh hopefully. And then
he brightened up suddenly. 'Anyhow,'
he said, 'it is nearly Luncheon Time.'
So he went home for it.

A PARTING THOUGHT ... YOU CAN'T EXPECT GRATITUDE IN LIFE, SO ASK FOR IT!

'If anybody wants to clap,' said Eeyore ...
'now is the time to do it.'
They all clapped.
'Thank you,' said Eeyore. 'Unexpected
and gratifying if a little lacking in Smack.'

About A.A.Milne

A.A.Milne was born in London in 1882. He began writing as a contributor to *Punch* magazine, and also wrote plays and poetry. Winnie-the-Pooh made his first appearance in *Punch* magazine in 1923. Soon after, in 1926, Milne published his first stories about Winnie-the-Pooh, which were an instant success. Since then, Pooh has become a world-famous bear, and Milne's stories have been translated into approximately forty different languages.

About E.H.Shepard

E.H.Shepard was born in London in 1879. He won a scholarship to the Royal Academy Schools and later, like Milne, worked for *Punch* magazine, as a cartoonist and illustrator. Shepard's witty and loving illustrations of Winnie~the~Pooh and his friends in the Hundred Acre Wood have become an inseparable part of the Pooh stories, and his illustrations have become classics in their own right.

COLLECT ALL FOUR BOOKS

WINNIE-THE-POOH
GLOOM & DOOM
FOR PESSIMISTS

A.A.MILNE
with decorations by E.H.SHEPARD

WINNIE-THE-POOH
DOUBT & DISQUIET
FOR WORRIERS

A.A.MILNE
with decorations by E.H.SHEPARD

WINNIE-THE-POOH

LITTLE SOMETHINGS
& SMACKERELS
FOR FOOD LOVERS

A.A.MILNE
with decorations by E.H.SHEPARD

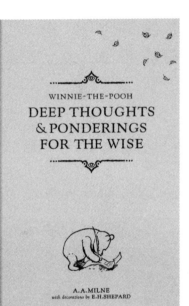

WINNIE-THE-POOH

DEEP THOUGHTS
& PONDERINGS
FOR THE WISE

A.A.MILNE
with decorations by E.H.SHEPARD